NO EASY TASK

Chloe Summers

A KISMET™ Romance

METEOR PUBLISHING CORPORATION
Bensalem, Pennsylvania

CHLOE SUMMERS

When she's not writing, Chloe Summers loves cooking, spending time with friends and enjoying life
with her husband, a corporate pilot and her daughter,
a teen model. She makes her home on the Jersey
shore and is an active member of New Jersey
Romance Writers. Her great passion is traveling to
exotic locales—Peru, the Ivory Coast and the Greek
Islands to name just a few.

ONE

Waiting! She'd had enough waiting in her life. "Not another minute," Doone Daniels muttered to herself, dropping the car keys into her beaded clutch and tucking it under her arm. Clenching a penlight between her teeth, she flipped off the overhead light and reached for the door handle as another clap of thunder vibrated through the car. She pulled the penlight from her mouth, pressed her nose to the rain glazed window and groaned. She'd actually enjoyed the challenging situations of the last six months, but to say she would enjoy what was just ahead would be stretching the point. Lightning flashed, throwing back the curious reflection of a pair of squinting eyes. *Definitely stretching it.*

Doone pointed the tiny flashlight at the sealed carton on the passenger seat next to her. She had no intention of dragging the bulky thing through the rain if there was a chance she'd misread the map. She picked up the umbrella and with a determined sigh shoved open the door. Rain pelted her face and upper body as she struggled to maneuver a half-opened umbrella into the darkness. The full blown fury of the Puget Sound storm whirled in, tugging it from her fingers. The umbrella skittered across the roadside clearing, then into the branches of a nearby tree. Catching sight of the umbrella's jaunty movements in the next flash of lightning, Doone's shoulders sagged. Snagged in the upper branches it was close enough to make out, but too high for any hope of retrieval. Well, she wasn't turning back!

She had no choice, not with Harry Shackley anxiously awaiting results at the office in Seattle. She pictured him, cigar in hand, gasping like a marathoner, as he'd rushed to the closing elevator and shouldered open the doors. "Forget that night job at Firebird's," he'd said, relieving her of her raincoat and tote bag, and shoving the carton into her arms instead. "I've got to get you on a ferry to Eagle's Island right away."

"What?! I'm late as it is and I have a bus to catch." She lifted the sealed carton away from her body, looked down at her ankle-length dress to her satin strapped shoes and laughed. "And I couldn't possibly go like this, Mr. Shackley."

The rotund detective waved his unlit cigar, effectively cutting short her protest. "Hunter Mackenzie has waited long enough for this. A thousand dollar bonus for your trouble, Daniels." He gestured with the wet end of the panatela as he smiled in what could only be described as a shark-like manner. "In cash," he added.

Had that insane conversation taken place only four hours ago? Ducking her head, she stepped from the rental car and kicked the door shut. Her toes instinctively curled against the cold water eddying through her panty hose and sandals. Harry Shackley had forgotten to give her back her raincoat and tote bag, too.

Twenty six years old and she was standing ankle deep in a mud puddle talking to herself. This night would be nothing more than a ridiculous memory once she opened the restaurant. "Money, you are doing this for the money . . . and the Emerald Light Cafe," she whispered aloud.

Doone repositioned the evening clutch under her arm and hitched up the skirt of the long dinner dress. Not the most appropriate clothing for her mission here tonight, she thought again. She winced as she pictured the bright red silk darkening in the rain. This wouldn't be happening if she'd left for her hostessing job five minutes sooner. Of course, if she'd done that, Mr. Shackley undoubtedly would have paid someone else for courier service.

Rivulets of mud and stones crisscrossed the steep incline as she started the climb, doggedly extracting one slender, mud-coated heel after the other. Never, in the two weeks that she'd worked for the Shackley Detective Agency, had she been asked to type or file, or even been allowed to answer the phone. And now this.

Lightning cracked across the black sky. She caught sight of a cedar shake roofline at the top of the hill. Lifting her hand to her forehead to block out the rain she continued to stare. The large house, she realized, had no lighted windows. The wind howled in again, catching her off balance and sending her sprawling onto a rocky outcropping. Her palms stung with the impact, but it was her side that had taken the brunt of the tumble. She allowed herself one cautious feel along her ribcage before pushing herself up and onto her feet. Ignoring the ache in her ribs, she grabbed up a soaking handful of skirt and continued her advance. What kind of a character was this Mackenzie to live out on a godforsaken road, miles from the only ferry terminal on Eagle's Island?

Five minutes later she leaned against a stack of firewood on Hunter Mackenzie's front deck and dropped the penlight into her beaded clutch. The welcoming scent of wood smoke filled her nostrils. With adrenalin still racing, she waited just long enough to catch her breath. No matter how crazy this overtime assignment might appear, it was more than worth it for the time the thousand dollars would buy. She glanced back into the darkness toward the hill she'd just taken. There'd been worse hills in life than that one.

She slicked back her hair, and with renewed determination, raised her hand to knock.

Inside the house Hunter Mackenzie's jaw tightened as he stared into the ragged-edged flames in the fireplace. He leaned forward in the rocker as visions of another evening began their determined path to his consciousness. Sooner or later he'd deal with them, purging them once and for all, but not now, not tonight. He rubbed the knot between his brows. Closer to the truth lay the unspoken "not ever."

A dark oath followed his coffee cup as he hurled it into the fire. He watched the liquid sizzle a second on a burning log, then vaporize in a satisfying hiss. Not a trace of it remained, not even a telltale scent that it had ever existed. If only the past could vanish like that, and the guilt . . .

The young Irish setter stretched out beside his rocker stirred in her sleep and thumped a glossy tail against his boot. Leaning down, he patted Sheeba's rump causing her to roll over and yawn delicately. The yawn ended in an ominous growl as the dog stood and looked toward the double doors. Hunter frowned slightly and shuffled the blueprints on the glass-topped trunk until he'd located his pipe and tobacco pouch.

The setter was less than a year old, at times overly playful and easily spooked. Hunter's father had insisted he take the pup, exclaiming at the time, "If you're not ready to let people back into your life, you can at least start with a harmless animal." That was one gnawed table leg, three mangled pipes, and too many holey socks ago. "Hush, girl," he said, tamping tobacco into the bowl.

Heedless of her master's command, the setter bounded toward the set of double doors, barking furiously. Then Hunter heard it. Two thunks. Picturing a fir bough splitting from a tree and falling to the overhang, he leaned back in the rocker.

"Sheeba, come. No one's fool enough to be out there tonight." There'd be a mess in the morning, but he'd have plenty of time to clean it up. He took another pinch of tobacco from the leather pouch and stared at it. Yes, he always had plenty of time.

Several distinct thunks came this time, and with them a muffled voice. "Hello?"

Hunter sat up suddenly. That rich, throaty voice . . . "Christina," he murmured. He rubbed at his mouth and mustache, then absently stroked his dark blond beard. Damn it, would she never leave him?

"Mr. Mackenzie, could you hurry please?"

Hunter gave a sharp twist to the pipe's stem then threw it onto the trunk. Of all the things he knew himself to be, crazy wasn't one of them. It couldn't be Christina out there. He did not believe in ghosts. Turning his head toward the set of double doors, he stood and listened, his nostrils flaring. There was someone out there, though, and that someone knew him by name. Well, whoever she was, she'd made a foolhardy mistake coming here tonight. Or any night, for that matter.

Pawing at the door, the young dog whined with excitement.

"Sheeba, go to your bed," he commanded as he approached the doors with quick, determined strides.

The dog ignored the command and only woofed impatiently for her master, now at her side, to open the door. Hunter cast Sheeba a disapproving look as he gently but firmly kneed her aside and reached for the doorknob.

Outside on the deck, Doone shifted her weight to one foot, then the other. Her shoulders were hunched up to her ear lobes. What was taking him so long to answer?

"Mr. Mackenzie, I have to talk to you, it's very important." She pressed an ear and shoulder to one of the doors and grimaced. Of all the insufferable nerve. She couldn't feel her toes any more and he was talking to that whining dog.

"I kn-know you're in there," Doone said through shivering lips.

A steely cold slap of rain soaked the back of her thighs, and with humiliating slowness seeped into the last warm spot on her body. Enough was enough. Doone kicked off a mud-coated shoe and snatched it up. She raised it to shoulder level, and steadied herself to pound it against the door. At that precise moment, the door jerked open, and the looming figure of Hunter Mackenzie filled the doorway.

The wind continued to blow, whipping the rain onto Hunter's face and flannel shirt with the force of a machine gun. He stared at the unfamiliar face before him, partly in astonishment, partly in relief. Christina would never have allowed herself to be caught in a rainstorm without a Burberry raincoat and matching umbrella. This shivering, disheveled woman definitely wasn't Christina.

"Who are you? What are you doing here?"

Before Doone could answer, the red setter, yowling with pleasure, bolted passed Mackenzie, dropped at Doone's feet and grovelled ecstatically. Doone's face froze in a half-formed scowl as she looked first at the animal, and then to Hunter Mackenzie.

The flickering light from the fireplace outlined his considerable height and the broad, rigid line of his shoulders, and provided an eerie nimbus through his thick curly hair. His left arm braced against the door jamb appeared to hold the very wall in place. Blinking away raindrops, she considered what to do about the effective barrier his arm presented. Getting past this man, if he were determined to keep her out, would be as easy as walking through the locked door of a bank vault. And his manner so far was as brutish as the storm.

Doone lowered her shoe to press it firmly against her breastbone. Squinting up into his shadowed face she spoke through clenched teeth. ''What I am doing here is freezing to death on your doorstep.'' She tried to control the shivering spasms wracking her body, but found it impossible to do. ''May I or may I not come in?''

His stare was riveted to the lush curves and draped hollows along the front of her body, and he fleetingly wondered what she looked like from the other side. Plowing his fingers through his light, wavy hair, Hunter finally stepped back. ''Yes, yes, of course,'' he said, impatiently. He may have pulled back from the world for awhile, but he wasn't about to let anyone freeze to death on his doorstep . . . with the possible exception of Harry Shackley.

Hugging her purse and shoe to her mid-section, Doone hobbled inside the huge, firelit room. Mackenzie had allowed just enough space to cross the threshold and inch a few steps to the left. She was now backed against the second door, virtually trapped. Woofing approval to her master, Sheeba chose that moment to worm her way through the door and past the two of them.

''To your bed,'' demanded Mackenzie.

Doone glanced toward the animal as it trotted two steps away and sat down, its pink tongue joyously displayed. A Doberman would have seemed a much more fitting pet for Hunter Mackenzie than this adorable, undisciplined puppy. Pressing her lips together to suppress a shivering burst of laughter, Doone returned her gaze to Mackenzie and his steel gray eyes. Enough dark blond hair covered his face to be called a beard and mustache, and not just a few days' growth. It was a look courted by certain young actors and too many terrorists, and until this moment she'd hated it.

Mackenzie's blatant stare continued. "You look like a raccoon," he stated flatly.

Doone rolled her eyes to the side. She caught a glimpse of a dripping lock of hair stuck to her cheek. Worse than a raccoon, much worse. She swallowed, dragging a knuckle under each of her eyes, hoping to wipe away the smudged mascara. "What do you have against raccoons?" she asked in a half joking manner.

He took a step closer and with a dangerously quiet movement reached above her to close the door. "Nothing. As long as they don't bother me, I don't bother them."

There was something paganly seductive about Mackenzie, from the light blond hair that tumbled to his collar, to the way he stood with his feet planted wide apart. And his eyes . . . From the anger behind the accusing look he'd leveled at her, she felt an unaccountable stab of guilt. No, that was wrong, she decided. Unease, certainly, but guilt? Mr. Shackley had pointedly warned her not to anger Mackenzie, but he appeared to be thriving on it from sources unknown. She challenged his stare with one of her own. But he wasn't to be intimidated that easily.

"I asked you who you are and what you are doing

on my doorstep at ten o'clock at night in the middle of a storm?'' With each word his face moved closer to hers.

The aura of power surrounding him had all but paralyzed her. His breath was warm and scented with espresso and if he came any closer she would be able to taste it on his lips. Her eyes closed at the extraordinary vision.

"Delivering . . . a package . . . to you," she finally managed.

His gaze slid down over the gown. He swallowed and shoved both hands into the pockets of his trousers as he stepped back. "You expect me to believe you work for a messenger service dressed like this?" he asked, as he continued to stare at the wet silk melded to her skin. Unless messenger services had changed drastically in the last year, legitimate messengers didn't deliver in ankle-length formals. Especially ankle-length formals that clung like wet tissue to every telling detail of her. . . . Then it hit him. He narrowed his eyes and drew back his head. Would the old man ever learn? Pushing a puppy on him was one thing, but he was definitely going to have words with his father over this. What was his father thinking of, sending him a woman?

"I know this looks strange, but I can explain everything. Just let me catch my breath," she said, sidling under his arm and away from him. He had the most peculiar way of taking all the oxygen out of the air when he spoke to her. That was how it felt, at least.

She backed across the room and bumped solidly into the sofa. The shoe and purse dropped to the rug as both her hands shot backwards for balance. Forcing a smile onto her lips she knelt down and scooped up her belongings.

"I'm moonlighting, Mr. Mackenzie," she said, rising, then dipping down again to pick up the fir needles that had fallen from the shoe.

"And that explains everything," he said, his eyes wide with feigned belief. He relaxed against the doors, crossing his legs and arms with the ease of a man once again in charge. She continued to move away from him using the back of her legs to guide her around the sofa. Raccoons, he decided, were never as graceful under pressure as this, and was he ever going to see her backside?

"Yes. No. I mean right before I was to leave for my night job, a message came in. I think he said from Washington, the other Washington." Doone watched as he nodded slowly. He had her babbling! A weak smile crossed her lips. "I haven't had this job very long and he pays very well and he lets me get dressed in the ladies room before I leave for my usual night job. He made it sound like a national emergency when he asked me to come here tonight, and I thought . . ."

"He?" Mackenzie's amusement slowly disappeared. This explanation was a bit fanciful, even for his father. So who else would send him a beautiful woman in the middle of the night? Or was she just a beautiful woman? That tingling sensation he hadn't felt since the old days started down his spine. He pulled himself erect.

"I'm from the Shackley Detective Agency, Mr. Mackenzie." She watched his lips thin out as he bared the edges of his teeth. For a moment he said nothing. The dog's tail had been slapping a steady rhythm against Mackenzie's pant leg, but stopped cold. As if sensing a change in her master, the dog slunk away to a far corner and flattened herself to the floor. The growing tension settled between Doone's shoulder blades with the prickling tenacity of a kitten's paw. Something was wrong.

"That bastard! Go back," he rasped, walking steadily toward her. "Go back and tell Harry this set-up won't work. That the Hunter Mackenzie he knew no longer exists."

Doone pushed a lock of hair from her forehead. "Look, I don't know what your problem is, but you're not going to tell me you aren't Hunter Mackenzie. I refuse to believe that." She shoved her hand into a side pocket of the gown and pulled out a soddened wad of paper. "This is a map to your house. Mr. Shackley drew it himself. Here, take a look," she said, peeling apart the paper.

Mackenzie snatched it from her outstretched hand and took it the few extra steps to the fireplace. He balled the ink smeared paper in his fist and threw it into the fire. Who the hell was she?! And why had Harry Shackley sent her tonight? He speared his fingers through his hair. "I want you out of here, lady. Right now."

Her eyes widened in exasperation. She hadn't slogged through that storm to meekly accept a case of bad manners as her reward. Tiger Daniel's daughter was made of tougher stuff than that and Hunter Mackenzie was about to find that out. She dropped the shoe and evening clutch onto the nearby sofa.

"Leave?" She hobbled toward him, motioning toward the doors with both hands. "In the middle of that mess out there? That's impossible. Besides, my car's stuck in the mud down there. I'll probably need a tow truck to pull it out."

She fumbled through her ruined topknot for two lacquer combs. They dangled over her ear before one slipped out and fell to the rug. She pulled out the other and motioned toward the doors with it. "I fell on that muddy mountain you probably call your driveway. I could sue you for that. And look at this dress," she demanded, tossing the second comb to the sofa. Doone made a feeble attempt to peel the drenched silk away from her thighs. "I need this dress for work." She pinched at the material again. "And it's not even paid for yet."

Immediately she was irritated with herself for attempting to explain any of this to him. She raised her chin, tilted her head, and stared at him. Surprisingly enough, his wrinkled brows indicated genuine curiosity. Slapping a hand to her collar bone, she began, "I could be making good tips right now, but am I doing that? No-o-o-o. I'm risking my life traipsing halfway across Puget Sound during a hurricane, or whatever this is, to get to you. Oh, gr-r-reat. Is this a rip in my sleeve?" Twisting her arm, she raised it toward him.

He leaned closer. "It's just the seam, I th—" His gaze suddenly flicked to her face. "Risk? Do you make these house calls . . . often?"

"You're my first," she said, while turning her arm for a better look at the damaged sleeve.

Leave it to Harry Shackley to shake him to his

bones with a professional as good as this one. She had a pretty convincing, but doubtlessly studied, naivete about her—something Harry had always strived for in the occasional call girl he hired. But not in his female agents. Hunter rubbed the back of his neck.

"How long have you been working for Shackley?"

She looked up, her bluster gone for the moment. "What? Oh, about two weeks."

So, she was a call girl. He wondered for a moment at the vague disappointment he felt, then shook his head. None of that mattered, he reminded himself, because he didn't care to know any of Harry Shackley's business. He was out of that life for good. Still, something was going down out there if Harry had sent her out spur of the moment on a night like this.

He studied her as she meticulously examined the other sleeve and then the rest of the dress. There was that inexplicable quality about her, though, that didn't ring true with what he now knew her to be. He scratched his chin. Maybe Harry had finally gotten lucky with this one—spunk, sex appeal, and an almost believable innocence that belied her primary profession. She was good, very good.

Taking off the other shoe and holding it over the fire screen, she shrugged as she picked several pebbles from the satin insole. "Let's be grown up about this. It's a simple business proposition. I've got something you obviously should have and with a little cooperation from you—" His indelicate snort caught her attention and her free hand formed a fist as it went to her hip. "Just what is so amusing?"

"Where the hell did Shackley get you from?"

She folded her arms across her breasts and felt the blood rush to her cheeks. He was as unpredictable as that howling wind outside. She had every right to be furious with this man. So it shouldn't matter that he found her so laughable, but it somehow did. Doone fixed her stare on the fire as a fit of shivering overtook her.

Mackenzie reached out to steady her, but at the last moment picked up the rocking chair and positioned it behind her. "You're not going to collapse on me, are you?" he said accusingly.

"That's not part of the plan," she assured him, sitting down in the well-padded rocker. She clasped her hands in her lap and hunched towards the fire. Right now the perfect plan for the Emerald Light Cafe felt about as firm as a soppy sponge.

Plan? Mackenzie went to an oriental cabinet on the opposite side of the room. His former case officer had managed to surprise him, he couldn't deny that. But the shock or the anger that Harry had hoped for wasn't going to happen now that he knew what Harry had done. Of course, his normal curiosity was another thing. Was she a contract local, or someone from back east near headquarters? "Are you from D.C.?"

"I lived there once," she said quietly. With my mother, when my father was in Vietnam, she wanted to explain. "A long time ago," she added in a soft whisper.

His palms flattened to the top of the cabinet. God, that voice, that throaty purr of a voice. He glanced over his shoulder at the probable local talent Shackley had hired. She was petting Sheeba's head with long even strokes. Hunter nibbled the inside of his cheek as he watched. When Christina was impatient with him she used to stroke her sable wrap like that. This woman bore a certain outward resemblance to Christina. She was tall, had dark hair, and a ready come back for everything he said. Yet, so strong was this stranger's presence that two seconds alone with her and the memory of Christina was melting away. For some inexplicable reason he envisioned a field of snow on a late winter morning with delicate patches of new growth breaking through.

Her toes were peeking out from beneath that torn, muddy hem. She looked so deep in thought, as if she were unaware of how perfectly seductive she looked in clinging red silk, her eyes bright, her slightly parted lips trembling . . . and all of her bathed in firelight. He shook his head wanting to believe it. He knew better, of course.

He turned back to the cabinet, deftly opened a bottle, and splashed brandy into two snifters. If he could just pin a label on her that would stick, he could stop this merry-go-round of desire and dread inside himself. Slowly he twisted the cork into the bottle and pushed it to the back of the cabinet. All right, so she'd managed to pique more than his idle curiosity. And she was here for a specific job. He lifted the snifters and turned toward her. It had been a long time since he'd taken a woman into his bed. Moments passed as he studied her profile. No amount of ruined makeup could dispel the fact that her good looks went beyond pretty. Any man could see that, he thought, staring at her perfectly lush mouth. He went to where she sat hunched in the rocking chair.

"You've had quite a night. Are you sure you're up to this?" he asked, as he handed her a snifter. He watched her enthusiasm return with a quick nod and smile.

That heightened blush in her cheeks . . . it had nothing to do with the cold, if he were not mistaken. Ah, yes, the heat of the moment. Wasn't that where he ought to have his mind and not on that haunting innocence that shone from her lapis-colored eyes? She was, after all, a call girl hired by Harry Shackley.

"You are a lovely one," he said, reluctantly shaking his head.

Doone watched, waiting. He wasn't quite smiling, but coupled with the hesitant warmth in his eyes, he might be on the verge. Under those copper tipped lashes, his eyes had softened to the color of nickel. He tucked a moist tongue into the corner of his mouth, and a sensation that could only be described as warmed velvet slid through her body. "Thank you. My name's Doone Daniels and I—"

Dune. Soft and warm. "It doesn't sound like the name of a . . ." his voice trailed off, watching the brightness build in her eyes. He silently cursed himself for the stupid slip. She was a professional, he reminded himself, and he wasn't just out of high school either. He took a deep breath and forced himself to watch the brandy swirl much too quickly in his glass. "How much is he paying you, by the way?"

Leaning back into the rocker, Doone brought the

glass to her mouth, sniffing the bouquet. Whatever had set him off before had all but vanished. Maybe they'd get through the next hour after all. She laughed quietly to herself and took a sip of brandy. The liquid heat flowed through her like a river of warm caresses. She rocked steadily. She was beginning to like it here. Stifling a yawn, she said, "It's a split payment, actually. Half for delivery of the documents down in the car, and the other half for—"

Hunter coughed half way through a swallow. "You left documents down in your car?" he said, swiping his chin with the back of his hand. He glanced toward the doors and then back to her. If he were Harry he'd have her hide for such carelessness.

She sipped at the brandy again before frowning up at him and shaking her head. "Really, no one but a duck would steal them on a night like this. If you don't mind my saying so, Mackenzie, you should learn to relax. I have every intention of fulfilling my commitment to Mr. Shackley. I've got a job to do, and considering what he's paying me, I'll make sure it's done and done well before I leave."

Was she always so glib? he wondered. He pressed his fingertips to the lengthy stubble on his cheek and felt vaguely disappointed for the second time since she'd arrived. Then his gaze locked with hers, but not for long. A man could fall into that look and never be the same. "We'll see," he said, watching her take a healthy swallow of his best brandy.

She eyed him carefully. "We certainly will. A thousand dollars is a thousand dollars. If you don't mind, I'd like to get this over with as quickly as possible. I haven't got time to waste on trips like this. Mind if I start off by asking you—"

"You charge a thousand dollars?" he asked incredulously.

"Look, you don't have to pay me. Mr. Shackley's taking care of that. And don't try making me feel guilty about the amount, either. This is the first job I've ever taken that entails going to a person's home, so this is all virgin territory to me." She shrugged. "Of course, considering the type of business Mr. Shackley's in, I don't think there's a standard fee, do you?" She looked up at him with the biggest blue eyes he'd ever seen. "Well, do you? Oh, never mind," she said, taking another slug from the snifter. "Not that it's any of your concern, but I really need that money. I'm going to open a place of my own."

The brandy was turning her usual throaty voice to a slow purr and she knew it. And couldn't have cared less. For the first time since she'd left the heated interior of the rental car, she was beginning to feel warm and relaxed. "I'm a highly creative person with substantial experience, but . . ." she continued rocking, "not quite enough capital at the moment. That's why I couldn't pass on the opportunity to show up here tonight."

The brandy was excellent. Too excellent, she thought, as it slid smoothly down her throat and seemingly right into her veins. If only she'd taken the time to eat, but Mr. Shackley had been almost manic about her catching the ferry.

"Tell me something." Hunter grabbed the top of the rocker and held it still. She twisted slightly to look up at him, her lashes fanning out to meet the smudges of mascara in a startling, yet endearing way. "Has Shackley tested your creativity personally?"

"You've got to be joking, Mackenzie. If you know Mr. Shackley, you know he's the fast food type." Her lips were tingling from the brandy and she licked them to bring back some feeling. "But you're not, am I right?" His eyes closed as he half coughed, half laughed his response. So she was right! She crooked a finger at him.

He came down on one knee beside the rocker. "Yes?"

She smiled confidently. "What I could do with . . . uh, this, for instance, would make your mouth water," she said, tapping the side of her glass.

"Brandy?" Had he understood her correctly? His lips pursed with interest as he allowed himself to wonder about the erotic possibilities that swirled in the bottom of the snifter.

She leaned towards him, sucking in air the moment her bruised ribs contacted with the hard arm of the rocker. "I've perfected this one thing. I haven't named it yet, but it's absolutely delectable. At least, I've been told that by half a dozen satisfied people. And once I open my place they'll be standing in line for it."

God, was he mad? His fingers racked the blond hair that hung halfway to his disbelieving stare. What the hell was he doing, entertaining the idea of letting her get on with her "business" here tonight? He reached out and set his snifter on the glass-topped trunk. She'd have to go, and fast. A shaker of nitroglycerine would be safer than the ongoing presence of this hauntingly beautiful creature. And he didn't need anything like this exploding into his life now. That was a certainty he could and would count on.

"That's it. You're gone." He jerked his glass from her hand and placed it with a snap beside his own. Then he stood and grabbed her wrists.

"Wait! What did I say?" Her bare feet slapped stubbornly against the floor as she fought the effects of the brandy and Mackenzie's strength both at the same time. "Will you wait a minute!?" But he wasn't listening. In the same moment he'd pulled her from the rocker. "Mackenzie! Please, please don't do this. Look, you don't understand. I've got to get that money for the Emerald Li—"

Suddenly he let go and she dropped down hard on the floor beside the rocker. For a moment he could have sworn it was Christina all over again. The way she had been in those days, begging him shamelessly.

"Don't beg, do you hear me? Don't you ever beg!" he shouted, grabbing her by the elbows and pulling her up against the length of him.

To Doone the heart wrenching passion in his voice seemed an element apart from the agile strength he used to haul her up. But she couldn't think of that now. He was heading her toward the door to throw her back out into the storm. Like a well-trained bouncer, he was avoiding any excess action or word as he half dragged, half guided her along the front of the sofa.

Mackenzie was instantly and agonizingly aware of his growing arousal now that he'd touched her. She was all wet sleekness and warm curves and surprising determination. Damn it. He couldn't want her. He had to get her out of his house and out of his mind. Completely.

"Just go, will you?"

"But I've got to do this. Why can't you understand?"

Frantic with the thought of losing out on the money, and thereby a perfectly beautiful but unpaid for neon sign, she ended up shouting into the hollow of his shoulder, "Don't you see? Mr. Shackley will just send someone else."

Hunter Mackenzie stopped dead in his tracks. Someone else? He felt part of himself tighten further as he watched her look up in confusion. Didn't she know what she was doing to him? He looked down on her dark hair already drying in curls around her head, and it was dark hair, not coal black like Christina's had been. This one smelled lightly of rain drenched flowers, and her mouth was . . . beautiful. He stifled a groan. She was wrong. There was no one else Harry Shackley could send. His hands relaxed allowing her to free her arm and then her entire body.

She stepped back, aware for the first time exactly how lightheaded the brandy had made her. Every place he'd been pressed against her felt licked by living flames. She drew her fingers across her forehead. No, that couldn't be right. The lingering sensation must have something to do with the brandy. She closed her arms protectively around her waist and avoided his stare. Maybe, for tonight at least, it wasn't such a bright idea to force him to listen. She kept her eyes on the tape deck, art objects, and rows of books in the cabinets behind him before she felt steady enough to speak.

"All right, we'll have it your way. I'll go."

She located her shoes and purse, gathered them up and then turned to face him. "I am coming back in the morning to finish this, Mr. Mackenzie. Now, if you'll call a taxi, you can be rid of me for the rest of the night." She attempted to straighten the sleeve of her dress, then realizing how futile any rearrangement might be at this point, gave a huffy sigh and dropped her shoes. Avoiding his eyes, she shoved her feet into them. "Mr. Shackley mentioned this Cliff Road Inn. Am I near it?"

Mackenzie shoved his hands into his trouser pockets, forcing away the image of her backside when she'd bent to gather up her things. It had been worth the wait. God, had it been worth the wait. He cleared his throat. "Shackley hasn't been totally straight with you. There's no taxi service on the island. Not yet. And as for the Cliff Road Inn, it's complete only on those blueprints." A jerk of his chin indicated a set on the trunk.

She rolled her eyes toward the ceiling fan and shook her head. Terrific, just terrific. Men never ceased to amaze her with their machinations and deceptions. She shook her head, swearing she'd never believe another word from any of them again. Look where one serious relationship had gotten her. So broke she'd had to resort to this! No wonder she was the first to leave any man who even remotely appeared interested in something more than friendship.

"It looks like I'm yours for the night, Mackenzie," she said. A hint of challenge returned to her voice as she added, "Whether you want me or not."

Wanted her? He tucked the tip of his tongue into the corner of his mouth. Yes, he wanted her. He was burning for her. He swallowed, knowing at that moment he had lost. And she had won. And maybe he had, too. He didn't know anything for sure right now, except that he needed air. He went to a coat tree near the door, plucked a lined windbreaker from it, and shrugged it on.

"You'll do." He whipped the zipper to his throat.

What did he mean by that? she wondered. He could be so obtuse. She wrapped both hands around the padded leather arm of the sofa and lowered herself to the edge of the cushion.

"Right now, I'm going down to your car to see what else you've brought me. I take it you have an overnight bag."

No, she didn't have an overnight bag. Mr. Shackley had forgotten to give her back her tote bag and umbrella, and once the ferry departed she couldn't go back to get them. Besides, for a thousand dollars she could sleep in her clothes for one night. A thousand dollars was a thousand dollars, after all. "It's really a mess out there. Maybe we could talk, maybe get a few things straightened out first?"

"Eager, aren't you? Sure we can talk. We can talk before, during, and after if you like. But first things first."

She sighed, easing back into the soft leather. If he was determined to get his hands on that package, who was she to try talking him out of it. Better to go along with him, she decided. A little graciousness at this point wouldn't hurt her position when it came to the other part of her job—convincing Hunter Mackenzie to meet with Mr. Shackley as soon as possible.

That might prove to be a little difficult considering his opinion of Mr. Shackley. She shoved back her fast forming curls with both hands and drew in a deep breath. She'd think about that in the morning. "Thanks for understanding my position. I never meant to disturb you, you know."

He raised one hand as the other reached for the knob. "No problem. If you're as good as you say you are, who knows, I'll probably be thanking you."

Her hands were still pressed against the sides of her face as her nose wrinkled in thorough puzzlement. "I'm sorry, Mr. Mackenzie, but I don't understand—"

"I'm not the kinky sort, but then I'm not a thoroughly conventional type either, and you've already disturbed me. Don't get too cozy on that sofa, we'll be using my bed. No use being uncomfortable in your work now, is there?"

The man was making no sense whatsoever. "Why would I be uncomfort . . . able in my . . . work?"

His decisive gaze passed over her once again, and this time she felt like an object under a microscope. Her heart thudded. My God! Of course. Those double entendres. How could she have been so stupid! "Wait a minute, you've got this all wrong."

"Let's be honest with each other, shall we?" he interrupted. "As long as you're here to seduce me, you might as well know my likes and dislikes where it involves sex. Bad temper is a turn off for me, but

I want you to know I'm willing to discuss this penchant of yours for brandy. Oh, and if you can get Sheeba into the kitchen and close the door, I'd appreciate that, too.''

The Irish setter gave a creaky yawn and began thumping her tail against the wall.

Forcing back a wave of panic, Doone jumped to her feet. ''Don't you dare leave this house until we've straightened this out, Mackenzie!''

''Patience, sweetheart. I'll be back as quickly as I can.''

Hunter shook his head in mock dismay as he watched Doone sputter in sheer frustration.

''I'd save my energy if I were you, Miss Daniels. It's been awhile, and you're going to need it.'' With that, he smiled and slipped quietly out the door.

TWO

A call girl! Doone stared at the door Hunter Mackenzie had just closed behind him. A thousand dollar a visit call girl, too. He had to be joking. Well, there were limits as to how far his joke could go. Pushing herself up from the sofa, she hurried across the living room and into the hall looking over her shoulder several times on the way. The bathroom would have a lock.

Once she'd found the bathroom and was inside it, she slammed the door, twisted the lock, and moved as far away from the door as she could. No need to panic. Nothing had happened. Yet. She pushed back her damp hair, then pressed both hands against her heart. His misconception simply had to be dealt with and explained away before anything did happen that would . . . embarrass them both.

Quite suddenly she sneezed. One hand immediately shot to her sore side, and she sneezed again. Great! Coming down with a cold was not part of the plan. And why did this bounty hunt have to center on such an arrogant, abrasive, self-centered, handsome—damn! Where did handsome fit in, anyway?

Nowhere. A handsome man fit nowhere into her plans now that the restaurant was about to become a reality. Especially not an arrogant, abrasive, self-centered one like Mackenzie. She grabbed a towel from the rack and began blotting her face and body. Exasperated by the little good it was doing, she bent over and began to wrap it turban-style around her hair. Her ribs ached from the awkward position and the feel of damp silk clinging to her body only added to the discomfort. Carefully raising her head, she caught the pained expression on her face in the medicine cabinet mirror.

"This is ridiculous! What am I doing here?!" she shouted to her reflection.

Why wasn't she in Firebird's foyer at this very moment hostessing to civilized patrons like she ought to be? Why was she shivering in some strange man's bathroom at ten thirty at night out on an island in the middle of Puget Sound? Was the Emerald Light Cafe really worth all of this?

That last question pulsed through her mind as she lifted a corner of the towel and rubbed at the smeared mascara around her eyes. Blue eyes. Tiger Daniels' blue eyes. They burned with waiting tears at the memory of her father. She eased herself down onto the rim of the tub and waited for the lump in her throat to dissolve.

Somehow the Emerald Light Cafe should have opened without her father having to take that civilian contract job. But he'd insisted that pushing back their plans for a few more years wouldn't matter if the Saudi Arabian flying job would give them a solid financial edge. A plan for the future, a family restaurant in Seattle, was the thing she must remember, he'd said. They'd been happy there that time he'd had shore duty. And they were going to be happy there again.

Her mother had brought up the idea of a Swiss boarding school. Doone had to agree the unique experience held far more appeal than the closed society of Saudi Arabia. Even so, as a military brat Doone had said too many goodbyes to Tiger Daniels, knowing each time that he might never return. She was reassured by the fact that the Saudi Arabian job was a civilian position, but the same empty feeling that was present with the previous goodbyes had suddenly doubled—her mother was going with him. Time, they'd told her, would pass quickly enough and she could expect lots of visits.

She swallowed the lump in her throat, only to have another one form. There *were* no guarantees in life. Eighteen months later both her parents were dead, and with them had gone the family future they'd dreamed about.

Doone had moved to Seattle after college almost four years ago, hoping to begin a new life while surrounding herself with the stuff of pleasant memories. Then six months ago because of the reorganization of the ad agency she worked for, she was forced to decide on a move to Chicago or lose her job. The promised promotion, pay raise, and relocation allotment suddenly paled when she thought about leaving Seattle, and that's when she discovered the family dream still alive within her.

She lifted her chin and sniffed loudly as she looked around her. Keeping her priorities in mind, she was shivering in Hunter Mackenzie's bathroom for a logical reason. She had a family dream to fulfill, and a plan to achieve that dream. The idea for the restaurant was just as viable today as it had been all those years ago.

As she pushed herself up from the rim of the tub, she spotted a thick terry robe hanging from a sturdy hook on the back of the door. Mackenzie was obviously not on a tight budget; the cost of drying this item alone would set her laundromat fund back at least three dryer loads.

The scent of soap and wintergreen liniment invaded her nostrils. She bunched the thick fabric between her palms, then caught herself sighing as she nuzzled the fabric. It would feel so good to pull it on and be completely warm and dry again. What an irresistible thought, she mused, slowly rubbing the material against her chin. Well, sooner or later he'd have to give her something dry to put on, and she wasn't getting any warmer in these wet clothes. Besides, waiting much longer in this condition was asking for pneumonia. She peeled off her clothing, throwing each clammy piece over the shower rod and reached for the robe. Slipping it on, she slowly closed her eyes and waited for the goose bumps to disappear.

Except for the persistent ache in her ribs and an impatient growl in her stomach, she was beginning to feel quite comfortable. If Mackenzie had a few aspirin in the medicine cabinet and something other than raw meat in the kitchen—his diet, most likely—the task of setting him straight would be bearable.

Five minutes later, she stood in Hunter Mackenzie's kitchen licking crumbs from her finger tips. It was rational, she told herself, to expect Mackenzie's libido to be dampened by the time he'd hiked up and down the slippery hill. All the same she realized she was clutching the thick lapels together at the thought of his return. She looked down at the bulky terry cloth and laughed. Nothing remotely resembling her female form could show through that.

She'd pushed a protruding cassette into the tape deck on her way into the kitchen and as it continued to play, she began to mentally review possible wall coverings for the Emerald Light Cafe. With the music from a Spanish guitar wafting through the house, the merits of rustic butter cream stucco walls began to outweigh the conservative stencilling she'd been so sure of yesterday. She scratched the side of her cheek and smiled to herself.

While living in Rota, Spain, with her parents they'd all agreed a Spanish touch to their future restaurant was a charming idea. Strange, it had taken this crazy escapade to Hunter Mackenzie's house to remind her of it. She took one last look around, and noticed that Mackenzie's red setter, who'd followed her into the kitchen, was sleeping soundly beside her water bowl. Doone backed out of the kitchen, quietly closed the door, and leaned her forehead against it. For just a second, the combination of the music, the sleeping dog, and the memory of her parents had somehow magically tricked her into believing that this was her home. That this was where she belonged. Although it lasted only an instant, it was the greatest feeling she'd had in years, and she wanted to hold onto it for as long as she could.

Hunter pushed open the front door and strode into

the house with a soggy carton in his arms. He dropped it to the floor and stared at his uninvited houseguest. Thick ribbons of dark hair had tumbled around her face and onto the towel over her shoulders. The gleaming, untamed arrangement only added to the startled look in her bright blue eyes. Why did she have to be so damned beautiful? For a silent moment their eyes met and held. Raising both his hands, he rubbed away the rain drops from his face and beard then looked her over again. What was it about a beautiful woman wrapped in oversized clothing that made a man want to— He gave the front door a casual kick shut. Gesturing to the robe she was wearing, he shook his head. "You make yourself right at home, don't you?"

Mackenzie's last twenty minutes spent out in the rain *had* dampened his ardor, but not his temper. Doone took several steps backwards, smoothed the front of the robe and said nothing. He had to appreciate the fact that she needed the dry warmth the robe provided; he was just being nasty again. She sighed. It was up to her to set the tone and he looked soaked to the bone. "You look like you could use some dry clothing, too."

"Turn it off."

She glanced toward the shelf that held the tape deck. Maybe she had made herself too at home. "I—it was sticking out of the tape deck. I didn't think . . ."

"Not my Segovia tape." He took off his jacket and turned to face her. "Your charming concern, Miss whoever-you-are. You can turn it off."

Doone tugged at the ends of the towel and slowly closed her eyes. She'd had it with this quarrelsome enigma. To think she'd actually been worried about him! She ran her tongue along the edge of her teeth and took in a deep breath. This was her opportunity to show Mackenzie she wasn't going to put up with his domineering, bullying attitude any longer, and she wasn't going to blow the chance by simply screaming at him, either. She lowered her chin and began, "You know perfectly well you would have given me dry clothes to put on as soon as you'd come to your senses, Mackenzie. I am not about to catch a cold or some- thing worse right when I need all my strength." She bent over and rewrapped the towel around her hair, stifling a groan when her ribs protested the movement.

"No, we can't have that. Post nasal drip has always been a turn off for me," he said.

When she raised her head again, she caught sight of him striding down the hall. Her painful wince ended in a grateful sigh when she realized he hadn't seen her hands shoot to her side. She needed him to think of her as an in-charge person, not a love-struck call girl turned klutz. By the sound of his last com- ment, she needed him to think it as soon as possible, too. She hurried after him until he disappeared into the bathroom. She sighed and rested her backside against the wall next to the door.

"Mackenzie, I didn't plan on being stuck here all night, and I really can't afford to get sick right now," she called to him through the partially opened door.

"And I suppose I can?" he asked. "By the way, how are you at playing nursie?"

"Now what is that suppose to mean?"

"It means I'm the one who will probably catch

cold because I'm now out of dry towels. And since you've claimed my robe—''

''I had to get out of those wet clothes sometime tonight.''

''I have to hand it to you, lady, you surely love your work.''

''Now, wait a minute.'' She started from the wall. ''I didn't mean it that way. . . .''

A tanned, masculine hand emerged from behind the bathroom door, dangling a pair of red bikini panties. ''That's not what these panties say.''

''I am *not* a call girl. Period! And do you mind?'' she snapped as she grasped the panties and tried to pull them out of his hand. He opened the door further and pulled her in. She didn't miss the flicker of amusement in his eyes as he allowed the elastic to stretch to its fullest measure before letting go.

He'd taken off his shirt. From the shadowed hollow of his throat to the rich patina of his belt buckle, crisp golden hair swirled over him like spun caramelized sugar. She swallowed nervously and reached to straighten her dress that was hanging over the shower rod. He was taking all the oxygen again. She was sure of it. She looked up. He wasn't even breathing heavily! His hands waited patiently at his hips. She *should* leave the bathroom, she thought, as her eyes strayed once again to his chest. ''You didn't happen to find my umbrella out there?''

''Sorry, Mary Poppins, I didn't. But you're certainly welcome to pour yourself back into that slinky red number and go out and search for it.'' Holding up his hand he continued, ''On second thought, forget it. I'm out of towels.''

He studied her a moment more. He liked her all breathless like this. Would her lips part just a little more if he touched them? Was this what she was like before she made love? He rubbed a thumb along his collar bone. Was she a hooker or wasn't she?! The walls seemed to close in a little as his gaze locked with hers. She could look like such a scared kid sometimes, and make him believe it, too. Shoving a hand through his hair, he quickly maneuvered around her and went out into the hall.

Doone returned the panties beside the rest of her drying clothing and followed him across the hall to his bedroom door. The door was flung wide open allowing her a good view of him bent over his dresser.

"Mackenzie?"

"Yeah?" He hadn't bothered to turn from his dresser.

"You've got to believe me, I'm really not a call girl. But I don't know how else to explain . . ."

Her voice trailed off as she focused in on a scar high on his left shoulder. The shiny scar resembled a thin, stiff ribbon angling up into a wider, ragged area. The thought passed through her mind that without the scar he would have been unbearably perfect, if such a concept were possible. His torso tapered smoothly from the wide set shoulders to a compact set of khaki clad buttocks and legs. Scar or no scar she had an overwhelming desire to touch him, to run her fingertips along the bronzed ridge of his shoulders, through the ruffled blond hair on his nape, and then down his spine.

Hunter pulled an undershirt from the dresser

drawer and used it to wipe his face and ears and the back of his neck while he studied her reflection in the mirror. What was it in those beautiful blue eyes of hers? Concern? Or curiosity? Revulsion at the extent of the disfigurement? He tossed the moistened shirt over a chair and pulled on a cotton knit crew neck. What the hell did he care what she thought? He'd have the scar for the rest of his life, but she'd be gone by lunch tomorrow.

He might as well get it over with, he decided. He turned to face her. "You had a question?"

Yes, she had a question. But by the vulnerable expression on his face and the defiant way his hands rested on his hips, she couldn't bring herself to ask it. Regaining her composure, she stepped into the doorway. "Yes, I do. Do you have any aspirin?"

He cocked his head, studying her. He had seen the question in her eyes, yet she hadn't asked it. Sassy, yet she knew when not to push. So there was sound intuition along with intelligence behind those spidery-lashed eyes. A gratifying sense of relief swept through him. Even the scar tissue which had been painfully protesting her presence seemed to relax.

"Don't tell me you have a headache," he said, a mischievous smile growing on his face.

There was no way to avoid telling him about the ache in her side now that she'd asked him for the aspirin. Doone shrugged. "No, as a matter of fact. It's my side. I must have fallen harder than . . . a *headache!*" she shouted. The temper she had sought to keep in check erupted again. "This little game of cat and mouse is about to end, do you understand?"

He pushed up the sleeves of his sweater and walked back to where she stood at the door. "I think we'll find a bottle in the medicine cabinet," he said, ignoring her narrow-eyed stare with infuriating pleasantness.

"You don't have any in there, Mackenzie."

With feigned exasperation he threw open his arms. "Well, I should have guessed you'd have already searched the place. What's it been? Let's see, less than an hour since you dropped by, isn't it? Leave it to Harry to pick a multi-talented type."

She stepped back into the hall and he followed her. Pointing toward the kitchen, he continued. "Perhaps you'd care to take a few moments to reconnoiter my kitchen. That is, if you haven't done so already." His eyes widened and his mouth remained open with mock surprise.

"I ate one of your apples," she mumbled. Too embarrassed to meet his eyes, she shifted her weight from one barefoot to the other.

He nodded. "An apple."

She scratched the side of her head. "And two Oreos. And a glass of milk."

His eyes widened again, and his taunting expression returned. "You ate my Oreos? I could sue you for that." He made a bowing gesture and swept his arm toward the living room.

"That's not funny, Mackenzie." She adjusted her towel, raised her chin, and started down the hall. "Mr. Shackley shoved me on the ferry so fast I didn't get a chance to eat dinner. And the snack bar on board was closed because of the weather." She stopped by the liquor cabinet and looked back. All six foot plus of him was casually leaned against the wall. His right leg crossed the left and the toe of his boot rested squarely on the light fir planking. His eyes were still sparkling with unused sarcasm.

"I'm trying like hell to be pleasant about this, Mackenzie, but you make it practically impossible."

"A thousand dollars can buy a lot of pleasantness these days," he said brightly.

"I have plans for that money. Legitimate and concrete. Your rudeness is exceeded only by your lack of imagination. And if you think you can intimidate me with your sorry attempt at humor . . . uhhhhhh!" Both hands had begun to reach for the slipping towel, but half-way there, they shot to her side.

He stood up, all semblances of sarcasm gone. "What is it?"

"Nothing," she gasped, ignoring the towel as it fell to the carpet. "Just that f-fall I mentioned. I hurt my ribs a little."

"Nothing?" That's all he needed, serious medical problems and no way to get her to a hospital. Frowning with uncertainty, he pulled at his collar, then pointed at her. "Look, it could be a punctured lung."

"Afraid I'll sue you? Come on, I think I'd know if I had a punctured lung," she said. She gave into the urge to glance down at her side, then back to him.

"You're going to have to let me check those ribs," Hunter announced with total conviction as he walked toward her. She stepped back toward the fireplace.

What exactly was he planning to do? she wondered. It was one thing to banter with him, but the misunderstanding about her career hadn't been cleared away and he wanted to play doctor. And she didn't have a stitch on underneath the robe. Her bravado disintegrated into unquelled panic.

"Don't you touch me or I'll—"

"Or you'll what? Scream? Am I really that frightening?" He reached out to catch the long tie encircling her waist and began to draw her to him with a careful, taunting slowness.

With grim resignation she allowed him to position himself squarely in front of her. What if she did scream? Might it arouse him? My God, she knew nothing for certain about this man—or about punctured lungs for that matter. Everything had been pure speculation concerning Mackenzie. Up until this moment dealing with him had been like playing a game. But suddenly there was no free space to run to. Mackenzie owned the board. And her ribs hurt like hell.

Hunter looked down at her open mouth and trembling chin. She was scared to death of him. He slipped two fingers under her chin and lifted it a fraction, stilling its movements. "I really don't want to frighten you, but do you understand the possible consequences of a punctured lung? If it collapses . . ."

Her eyes widened with panic that made his heart cringe.

Looking into his eyes was like falling off a cliff with no promise of a safety net at the bottom. "Mackenzie?"

"Yes?"

"Mackenzie, do you have medical training for this?"

"I do. Now let's get this over with."

"Mackenzie?"

He sighed. "What?"

"Mackenzie, I don't, uh, have anything on under this."

He chewed the inside of his cheek, forcing himself not to smile. "I understand," he said with childlike simplicity. "Now if you'll be quiet—"

"Mackenzie?"

"Is this your last question?"

She nodded. "Mackenzie, can you die from a punctured lung?"

His eyes snapped shut. Pictures of Christina lying slack in his arms floated eerily through his mind. "You're not going to die," he said quietly. His eyes stayed shut for a long time. When he opened them again, he gently peeled her fingers from the tie. With one hand pressed gently against her lower spine he slipped the other inside the bulky drape of the terry cloth.

"Breathe," he demanded. "Hmm. Just breathe normally."

" 'Hmmm?' What does 'hmmmm' mean?" Doone's eyes fixed on one of the ceiling fans as she tried to ignore the heat of his fingertips. He was being gentle, so very gentle with her. That was nice. Reassured, she relaxed and closed her eyes. This wasn't so bad. She sighed, then felt her breath catch. What was this pleasure that shimmied through her body? Images of them both locked together in an intimate embrace teased at her mind. Let him play the good doctor and finish. Yes, let him finish soon.

Now what was he doing? The fleshy pad of his

thumb lightly grazed the swell of her breast once, twice. . . . A small whimper escaped her constricted throat. Betrayed by her own body, was there no justice in the world?!

"Did that hurt?" he asked.

"No, yes . . . no." Torture was more like it, and it had nothing to do with the soreness in her side.

"Aren't you through yet?" she asked with as much calmness as she could muster.

"No. Hold the robe together." Her eyes flicked open as she grappled to catch the robe both above and below his hand.

Hunter looked away as he shifted his stance to allow both hands inside the robe. They glided slowly, expertly down her rib cage and came to rest in the well-defined curve of her waist.

"Probably just bruised," he reported with relief. "You'll be a little sore tomorrow." As his eyes met hers his fingertips rapidly traced the feminine flare of her hips. "Now, now, don't take it too hard," he said, withdrawing his hands and resting them on his own hips. "We'll work around the soreness."

With one wide step she distanced herself from him and arranged the robe to resemble a monklike wrap.

"If you could control yourself for just a second, Doctor Mackenzie, I'm going to tell you for the last time, I'm not a call girl. And—"

"Oh, is that so?" he cut in. He reached down and picked up the towel, shoving it into her upturned palms. "Am I supposed to believe that when you come into my home looking like a contestant for a wet T-shirt competition?" he asked half seriously.

"I didn't have a chance to change. I was already

dressed for my night job at Firebird's and was headed out the door when he caught me. Why can't you believe me?''

Slowly he circled her and then took up his pipe and gestured with it as he spoke almost angrily. ''Night job? Sure, that I can believe. You're parading around my house attempting a seduction in nothing but my bathrobe and your earrings. Did Harry give you those or was it some other customer?''

If he only knew what her sexual experience had been! Her hand came toward his face like an arrow shot from a taut bow. With the reflexes of a jungle cat Hunter dropped the pipe. His flattened palm shot forward to fend the blow.

''How dare you!'' she whispered, as tears brimmed her eyes and splashed onto her reddened face. ''I've never met a meaner, ruder, more uncivilized brute in all my life. Seduce you?! Are you out of your mind? I'd rather seduce a polar bear,'' she added, ''and I'd probably enjoy it more.'' Slapping away the humiliating flow of tears, she continued. ''If you can't see beyond the immediate circumstances, no matter how questionable they appear, then you are one hell of a failure as a, a . . . gentleman.''

''Damn questionable circumstances,'' he muttered, experiencing a small pang of guilt as he watched her bring the trembling chin under control. She'd been through a lot tonight and was still having to contend with him. He looked away, knowing he'd pushed her too far. ''All right, what do you have to say for yourself?''

Her gaze shifted to the carton he had dropped by the door on his return. ''You can forget the Doone

Daniels factor in this," she began as she watched him reach down to pick up his pipe. "I'm supposed to deliver that carton to you and then see to it that you show up at the agency by tomorrow evening. That's all he told me and that's all I agreed to," she said, taking a few steps to the sofa. She sat down carefully and began to rub her temples. "Will you come back with me? I have to know." She licked her lips, dreading his possible refusal.

Hunter sensed her nervous gaze on him as he knocked the pipe against the mantel. "What's so important that you'd get involved in what you yourself call a questionable set up?"

"It's a long story that would probably bore you," she said wearily.

He fought back a smile. "Probably, but if you insist on not seducing me, you might as well tell it." He turned around to face her. "I might be more willing to cooperate with you if I knew where you were coming from."

She studied his face for a moment and then leaned back into the sofa. "I moved out here from Boston some time ago to work for an ad agency. Everything was great," she said with a shrug. Come to think of it, everything hadn't been great. Safe, uneventful, and uninvolved but not great. Despite Seattle's handsome supply of eligible bachelors, her basic trust in men hadn't returned. Not after the broken engagement.

"Go on," he urged. He watched as she refocused on him and the fragile smile that came over her face hit him with surprising force. Suddenly, he ached to know everything about her.

"You know Seattle has a reputation for producing the most inventive local beer commercials in the country. The ad agency I was working for picked up a national beer account and decided to reorganize and relocate. That was about six months ago. It forced me to make a decision about some, uh, long-term personal goals."

She sighed and folded her legs under her. She might as well tell him, it couldn't do her position any harm, and it might even help. "It made me remember the real reason I'd come back to the area in the first place. My family had planned to open a restaurant in Seattle after my father retired from the military." She looked up at Mackenzie and saw him rest an arm along the mantel. He nodded for her to continue.

"Well, unless you're a military brat, you can't imagine how much that plan meant to me. We were going to be together, all of us." She brought a white knuckled fist to her chest. "Mother and I wouldn't have to say goodbye to my father ever again and know that he might never come back." She relaxed her fist and dropped her hand to her lap. She took a moment to fight down the inevitable lump in her throat. "But that didn't work out. Anyway, the opportunity to break from my job was just that, an opportunity. I wanted and still want that restaurant. But I'm running out of time."

"Time?" Mackenzie repeated. What did she know about time? God, there was plenty of it. Endless circles of time, all leading back to a yesterday he couldn't get away from.

"I quit that job six months ago and have been

working full tilt toward the restaurant. I've been working two jobs. Well, three actually, with the dance classes at Marta's. She's my landlady and very good friend.''

"Three jobs?'' He ran his hands through his hair. "When do you sleep?''

"Sleep? I can't think about sleep, Mackenzie! I've got less than three weeks to come up with ten thousand dollars.''

"What about a loan?''

"You ought to know how difficult small business loans are to get any more. Or maybe you didn't need one for your inn,'' she said, casting a glance at the blueprints. "Anyway, I've already used my savings.''

To be totally honest, Bailey Swift had used most of the money just before he disappeared to Florida. The humiliating incident had happened in the year after her parents' death when her childhood fear of abandonment had returned. Bailey Swift had promised a future of togetherness, and, incidentally, a great investment opportunity in his ''sister's'' proposed chain of hair salons. That's when her family lawyer Cam Ludlow stepped in to explain the real Bailey Swift. She blew softly through her lips, surprised at the strong need within her to hide the old embarrassment from Hunter Mackenzie. She continued. "There was tuition at the culinary institute. Oh, and the down payment on the neon sign alone took quite a chunk. Then there were the monogrammed dishes, kitchen ware, and the best imported espresso machine I could get. I figured out with the bus system I could do without my car, so I sold that, too.''

"Are you always this impatient about things you want?"

"It's more than a thing, more than a business, Mackenzie. Oh, never mind, you wouldn't understand. It all has to do with the past, with things left unfinished, with a part of me left incomplete. I want something to call my own, Mackenzie. Something I don't have to fear disappearing on me. Like roots, like . . . family." She swallowed, surprised at how much about herself she'd revealed to him. "I'm not waiting for miracles any longer," her voice trailed off. He wasn't saying anything, only fiddling with that damn pipe of his. Not only didn't he understand, he probably thought she was crazy playing it so close to the edge financially.

"I'm not as scatterbrained as you might think. I've been in contact with our . . . my attorney. Cam's been working at selling some property of mine back in Boston. As soon as it sells I'll be fine. It's just that this chance at the loft space at the Public Market came up so suddenly, and Cam's been a little hard to reach—"

"Cam?" He raised his eyebrows.

"We're very good friends. He's been like an older brother."

"I get the picture."

"No, you don't get the picture." She fingered her side. Cam *was* like a big brother. The only reason conversations concerning her business affairs were held in unlikely places lately was his genuine big brotherly concern. He'd always taken extra interest in her welfare and probably just felt a little sorry for the present financial situation she was in. After all, a tour of a winery, dinners at the best restaurants in the city, and an evening cruise around Elliott Bay on his associate's yacht were nothing to be suspicious about. In fact, except for the tour of the winery, Cam planned most of their time with local politicians.

Giving Mackenzie a squinty eyed look, she pursed her lips. Doubt Cam Ludlow's motives? Ridiculous, even if Marta didn't like him.

"Hmm. And Shackley, how did you get involved with him?" His voice rose slightly as he walked across the room and into the kitchen. The dog whined in delight, then barked sharply. "Down, Sheeba, stay."

Doone waited for Hunter's reappearance before she answered. "As soon as I made the decision to open a restaurant, I started spending what money I had to set things in motion. Things got tight quicker than I thought and I began searching the want ads for something to get by with until I could talk to Cam. My job with Mr. Shackley, especially his offer tonight, was a miracle."

"I'll bet. Here, take these," he said, as he handed her two aspirin tablets and a glass of water. "So you got yourself hooked up with the likes of Harry Shackley because you had a warm feeling about a little restaurant that somehow's going to make your life complete? Drink all of that, it's good for you."

"Little, Mackenzie? As in insignificant, hobby-like? Or, as in, not the size of IBM or an oil cartel?"

"The latter."

"That little restaurant might not sound like much to you, but it is to me. I'll have complete control of it. It's something I'll be able to count on being there. Can't you understand that?''

He understood all right. People had the nasty habit of dying on you. But a business of your own was something else. Even if it burned to the ground, it could be rebuilt in a matter of months. And what had you lost but time? There was always plenty of that. "Tell me, weren't you a tad suspicious when he hired you just like that?" he asked, snapping his fingers.

"Well, yes, I . . . how did you know?"

"I know Harry. Go on with your story."

Glancing sideways to study his attentive stare, she tilted her head. "Are you patronizing me?"

He dragged the tip of his index finger along the smooth plane of his bottom lip and gave careful consideration to his next words.

"Miss Daniels, you're being used."

"I'm picking up on that," she replied. "And I can see you're anxious to tell me how, so go ahead. You have a captive audience." She reached into her evening bag which was still lying on the sofa where she'd tossed it earlier. With a flickering glance in his direction, she dumped the contents of the little purse out onto the sofa, pulled out a hairbrush, and then reloaded the purse.

Hunter watched in silence. The contents of Christina's purse had never ceased to amaze him. But this one had a personality all its own. A wallet, a penlight, a weird looking hairbrush, a notebook, a package of cupcake papers, and a meat thermometer. As he watched her begin to brush her hair, he tried to figure out what, besides a microwave oven, was missing from the list.

She carefully brushed back the sides and top leaving the damp mass to cluster around her shoulders. It reminded him of the sable wrap bunched to Christina's ears when she'd gotten her way. But somehow this girl's cheekbones weren't quite so angular and . . . .

"Well . . . ?" she asked.

Then it came to him. Doone didn't carry cosmetics and she didn't carry a gun. He cleared his throat and looked away for a moment before he spoke.

"First of all, you take heed of an ad written to bring in as many pretty, young, and desperate girls as possible. 'Secretary/girl Friday to busy detective. Opportunity for big bonus payments,' or something along that line. Am I right?"

Squirming at his on-target review, she nodded.

"When you arrived for the interview the office was probably filled beyond the local fire code capacity with some very attractive young ladies."

"Well, yes," she replied, burying her fingertips in the curls that spilled over her shoulders. This was no shot in the dark. Mackenzie had it nailed. "Will you get to the point?"

"The point is, as soon as he gets a good look at you and finds out what dire straits you're in financially, he hires you. And you weren't even asked if you could type now, were you?"

"Did he make a video tape or something? What's this all about?"

"A con. Shackley is not a detective."

"What? Why of course he is. He has an office with Shackley Detective Agency printed in gold right on the frosted window. He even acts like a detective.'' Whatever that meant, she thought to herself. ''Don't you dare stand there with that snide look, Mackenzie.''

''The gold paint is, like the areas behind your ears, still wet.''

That familiar sinking sensation started in her chest. He was telling her the truth and she couldn't just wish it away. She swallowed.

''What was I supposed to do, look him up in the phone book, call the Better Business Bureau?''

''Damn right, you should have,'' he shot back.

''I've got deadlines, Mackenzie! I need the money. Who is Harry Shackley, or what is he?''

''He works for the government, tracking down dope dealers, big dope dealers.''

''Oh, my God! He's tracking you down?'' she asked, wide-eyed. She felt the color begin to drain from her face and her mouth go dry as she watched him sit calmly down beside her. He tamped the tobacco into his pipe. He lit it and looked up.

''No,'' he finally said, and she let go of the breath she'd been holding. ''Up until a year ago I worked for that same agency. I don't any more, but he refuses to accept that fact. He thinks there was some unfinished business when I resigned. Unfinished business—and listen carefully, lady—that I'm not involving myself with further. I'm an innkeeper,'' he said, glancing in the bowl of his pipe. ''Or will be soon enough. So, you see, I can't come back with you.''

If he didn't return with her, there'd be no money, no lease, and no Emerald Light Cafe. The mere possibility of another person renting that loft overlooking Elliott Bay unnerved her. She had to try something fast to rectify the finality of his answer. She bit the inside of her cheek until it hurt. Although he wasn't some irate customer at Firebird's, maybe she could charm him into reconsidering. Or should she even try? He wasn't complaining about the lack of cocktail sauce for his shrimp, he simply didn't want to see Harry Shackley. She had to try, there was nothing else she could do. Pressing both hands onto the cushion next to her, she leaned towards him and gave him her most sincere smile.

"Well, of course, if you don't want to work with him any more, he can't make you. No one can. But it would mean an awful lot to me if you could just show up at that office tomorrow. Perhaps if you told him in person he'd be more inclined to believe you this time. Sometimes people must be told straight out and, uh . . ."

This approach was failing, definitely failing. He hadn't even bothered to meet her gaze. As a matter of fact, he'd picked up the blueprints and stuck his nose in them the moment she'd smiled at him.

Doone began grunting her way up off the sofa.

"Careful," he warned, not bothering to look at her.

Ignoring his warning, she made it up. She moved in front of him, and crinkled down the top edge of his blueprints with her fingertips.

"I'm guessing you have some sort of personal aversion to Mr. Shackley, but enforcing drug laws or smuggling or whatever it is is still a noble endeavor. Perhaps his manner of operating may not be your style, it's certainly not mine, but you have to believe he's doing it for a good cause."

"Well, aren't we the little hymn singer tonight?" he said, crumpling the blueprints halfway to his lap. "Listen up, because I only want to say this one time. I've known him since Tehran and he only gets worse. Shackley's pursuing this as his last big flash before he goes out to pasture with his fat pension, and some questionable investments, not to mention a condominium in Jamaica." Folding the blueprints in crisp, precise sections, he slapped them onto the glass-topped trunk. The determined action caused her to move back, and he took the opportunity to stand up. "Don't kid yourself, he usually gets the job done, but his true character stinks. And he's a dangerous person when it comes to pretty women, too. Pretty and very naive. Now let's talk about something else."

"You know what I think, Mackenzie? I think you're just trying to frighten me."

"More Oreos and milk? Or something a little stronger? Hot chocolate?" he asked, ignoring the intensity of her gaze.

She'd placed her hands on her hips and was soundlessly tapping her fingernails against them. "I don't want a drink. I want some answers. Correct me if I'm wrong," she continued, recapturing the pace of her questioning, "but isn't there some contract you haven't fulfilled, or some code of honor you seem so hasty to ignore?"

He took a deep breath and let it out slowly as he turned from her and walked over to the fire.

She'd taken a chance at losing her hostessing job for a full thousand dollars, not the five hundred she'd get if Mackenzie didn't come back with her. She had to keep trying. "Well, don't you think the least you could do would be to look at what's in the carton?"

"There's nothing in there I want to see," he murmured, staring into the fire.

"Then I'm sure you won't mind if I . . ." she began as she started for the carton.

"No!" he shouted, whirling around and pulling the pipe from his lips all in the same moment.

She stopped and slowly turned to look at him. He didn't know if it was the "I won" smile on her lips, or the challenging gleam in her eye, but Hunter snorted his surrender. Swearing under his breath, he pulled an ornate letter opener from the shelf near the tape deck and joined her near the door.

"We'll see what Harry thinks is so important that he sent this little lamb to slaughter for it."

"Isn't that a rather weak metaphor for a wet T-shirt contestant, Mackenzie?" she asked, clasping her hands behind her back.

A slow grin passed over his face and he nodded once. He'd liked to have laughed, but their shared grins were enough emotional intimacy for him to handle now. He couldn't remember the last time he'd looked into a woman's eyes and shared a good laugh. "Touché," he finally said and squatted down. The ivory elephant adorning the hilt of the letter opener raced across the top of the carton.

Doone reached to assist him.

"Not so fast," he cautioned.

"Excuse me, I didn't mean to pry," she said with no small amount of embarrassment. After all, patience was a virtue, and it was time Hunter Mackenzie thought of her as virtuous, sort of. No, that was wrong. Virtuous, definitely virtuous.

"Hmm," he peered first into the carton, then to Doone who was clasping and unclasping her hands. "A thousand dollars?"

She shrugged as she cast a glance toward the carton.

"The possibility never occurred to you that something might be illegal or immoral with this little caper if Shackley was willing to pay that high a price?"

"I assumed he was licensed, Mackenzie. Seattle's a rich town with lots of capital." She sighed wearily. "But you're right, I guess I was eager to accept it as a gift horse sort of situation."

"Speaking of gifts, I think your boss has another here for you."

A puzzled look crossed her face. "What in the world . . . ?"

Mackenzie drew out a short, black negligee. He blew on the black ostrich feathers along the neckline and carefully inspected the net shrouded slits that descended from each arm opening. Holding the article just out of Doone's reach, Hunter eyed it with a cocky wariness. "Then again, he probably had me in mind, too. What do you think?"

"I'll throttle him, I swear it," she said, tearing the negligee from his raised hand. With it bunched inside her fists, she squared her shoulders and hurried to the hearth. She threw the sleazy nightgown into the fire and watched it flame. "He actually thought I would wear that disgusting thing. Can you imagine?"

"Oh, I have a pretty good imagination. Contrary to your belief," he murmured in reply as he pulled out several thick file folders, stacked them on the floor and reached in to withdraw the manila envelope marked EYES ONLY. He slit it open and withdrew a thick, official looking document.

Doone pursed her lips and narrowed her eyes at him. He had already begun to read the document and didn't catch her irked expression. Absently he touched his fingertips to his mustache and then his hair roughened jaw. It was as if she'd been wiped from the face of the earth. Minutes ticked by. He walked to the edge of the sofa and sat down on its rolled arm.

"Mackenzie, is something wrong?"

He lifted his gaze from the paper and refocused his eyes on her face. She saw the deeply etched lines around his eyes as he looked up. He seemed to have aged ten years in the last few minutes.

"Your honor was never in danger. I . . . won't bother you, I assure you," he spoke hoarsely.

The gravity in his voice made Doone anxious, not for herself, she realized, but for him. Her fingertips went to her breastbone as if something sharp had just scraped her heart. She was suddenly and acutely certain that whatever it was she had brought to him was pivotal in his life.

He returned his attention to the document, his brow furrowing in renewed concentration.

Learning about Hunter Mackenzie was like riding an endless emotional roller coaster. Around every curve was another surprise. Each one holding a new depth or height never imagined and never explored before. Who was this man and just what was it about him that, despite the incredible jerking around her emotions had undergone in the last hour, intrigued her to continue the adventure of knowing him? What had she unleashed by coming here tonight? She realized with a sense of urgency that nothing was ever going to be quite the same again. For either of them. She was certain of that, certain beyond a feeling, certain beyond intuition.

Sensing her stare, Hunter gave in to the urge to look into her face once again. He'd give her credit for not being obsessive about demanding an explanation. Harry was a lucky bastard to have found her. But, he wondered, am I? He considered the question as he continued to watch her. She was staring into the fire, all wrapped up like some precious butterfly in a terry cloth cocoon.

"I have a lot of reading to do. Go ahead and use my room, I won't be needing it tonight," he told her. The puzzled expression on her face told him more about the concern she had for him than any words she could have spoken. "Please, just go to bed." She finally nodded and went down the hall to his room and quietly shut the door.

Another hour passed before he tugged off his boots and stretched out on the sofa. An exhausted Hunter Mackenzie gave the pillow several soft punches before easing his aching shoulder into it. He pictured the look in her eyes right before she'd turned to go to his room. "You were perfect for the job, Doone Daniels. Absolutely perfect," he whispered.

THREE

Hunter readjusted the Velcro closures of his work gloves and inhaled the cool, morning air. The spring-scented air along Portugal's southern coast had been as seductive, but never as vital as it was here in Puget Sound. Portugal. He closed his eyes, giving in to images of the carefully tended grounds around the casino. He'd always known Shackley wouldn't give up on getting him back into place in Albufeira. And from the cable traffic he'd read last night, Shackley now had reason to hurry. Christina's killer was spotted three weeks ago in Albufeira attempting to reestablish a trafficking network for his heroin.

He opened his eyes and picked up the axe resting against his leg. Christina was dead and he couldn't bring her back. He was out of that world they'd belonged to, no longer inspired to snare another drug dealer, no longer determined to keep up his cover as casino manager, and no longer responsible for other people's lives. Why in hell should he even consider going back? Hunter brought the axe high above his head and then swiftly downwards into the cleft of a half split log.

Who was he trying to kid? An opportunity to avenge Christina's death couldn't be discounted. He needed time to think.

First thing this morning, he'd send that long-legged, blue eyed butterfly back to Seattle with specific instructions for Shackley to stay put. He raised the axe again, half smiling at the memory of her confessing to eating those Oreos. There was something about her, something that brought the loneliness of the last year into crystal sharp focus and then muted it. Hunter's shoulders heaved once again. The impact of metal against wood produced an echoing thunk that ricocheted deep into the surrounding forest.

The morning sounds of Eagle's Island softened as the realization came to him: He couldn't let Doone Daniels go back just yet. Harry Shackley had used a trump card when he'd chosen her, a civilian, as his courier. If she returned to Seattle today without him, Shackley would come himself. Hunter kicked aside the wood at his feet then methodically balanced another log on the block. He didn't want Shackley out here like some sniffing hound dog, forcing him up a tree or off the island until he was damn good and ready! He chopped solidly into the next piece of wood.

Frightening her was the last thing he wanted, but she had to be told she wasn't going back to Seattle for a while. He chopped again. Not until he figured out if he wanted back in on an operation that had already taken one life. Two pieces of wood thumped onto the springy wood chip carpet surrounding his boots. Silence replaced the echoing thumps.

He swiped at the perspiration on his forehead. God knows, he could use a little company. There. He'd admitted it. But that didn't mean he ought to or had to get involved with her. He placed the last piece on the block and stepped back. After all, he mused, lifting the axe high above his head, if he could put a government agency on hold for nearly a year, he most certainly could remain aloof from one silken-skinned, purry-voiced, blue-eyed female. If he wanted to. A cool breeze blew across his back and shoulders, mingling with the already sensuous feel of the hot sun there. In that instant the image of Doone Daniels, stripped to the waist, pressing against his back and whispering erotic demands against his ear, drifted through his mind.

Doone walked out of the house with a slow but purposeful stride. This morning she had unfinished business to conduct with Hunter Mackenzie. She glanced up from the two full mugs she gingerly carried and stopped. Hot coffee threatened to dribble over the rim of each mug and down the front of the terry robe. But she barely noticed because all of her attention was focused on the sight before her.

He was standing in the sun-splashed clearing with his back toward her, stripped to the waist. Sunlight was shafting through the firs and glistening off his sweat slick skin. The shifting patterns of light along his back and shoulders held her spellbound. Scar or no scar, he was beautiful. From his tousled hair to his well-worn hiking boots, he was a work of art that was making her throat ache. She swallowed and forced herself to recall why she'd stepped out on the deck in the first place. The ferry was arriving in a few hours, and she had to convince him to be on it when it returned to Seattle.

"Good morning," said a cheery voice from the deck. "How do you take your morning coffee?"

This time the axe missed its mark by a good six inches. Hunter swallowed and reached to reposition the wood. If morning fantasies could come true, the whispered demands would have a raspier quality as they vibrated through every fiber of his body. He wrenched the axe free from the chopping block.

"Excuse me. Remember me? Owner of the artfully tattered red gown?" Even though he hadn't yet turned around, Doone held up a mug. "Sugar?" She had determined that once he turned around, put on his shirt, and had a cup of coffee, the dryness in her mouth would be gone. Then she could get to work on ferrying back to Seattle with Mackenzie in tow.

Hunter stepped back from the chopping block. How was he going to tell her, and why did she sound so happy? He was never happy in the morning. Given to impulsive actions occasionally, he admitted, wincing, as he brushed the canvas glove along his freshly shaven cheek. At five thirty this morning, it had definitely been impulsive.

Doone glared at his back. " 'How did you sleep last night, Miss Daniels?' " she said in an affected masculine growl. She supplied the answer in a cordial but somewhat clipped tone. "Just fine, thank you."

When he didn't respond, she sighed quietly. Sitting down on the top step she placed one of the bright orange mugs half-way across it. If he wasn't a morning person, she could understand that, but he could at least turn to face her and acknowledge her presence. Out of the corner of her eye she watched him tug off the ragged canvas gloves and rub them against his sweat-soaked brow. Then with obviously well-practiced, precise movements he made a slow circle with his scarred shoulder.

After working out the lingering stiffness, Hunter piled the split logs into the log carrier and brought them to the deck. Without missing a beat, he reached for the navy polo shirt lying next to the stack and slipped it over his head. He rimmed each short sleeve with his fingers, stretching the openings a fraction wider to accommodate his biceps. How, in the name of heaven, was he going to tell her she was staying without having her fly off the handle?

He focused on a diamond bright fringe of raindrops dripping from the edge of the deck. "How are your ribs, uh, June, isn't it?" He knew damn well her name wasn't June.

She gave a quick, disbelieving look out to nowhere.

Hunter glanced at her and saw her profile framed in the most glorious riot of chestnut curls he'd ever seen. There was a faint dusting of freckles across her slightly upturned nose. And she was trying her damnedest not to look at him. Ignoring her for so long, he decided, wasn't his brightest move of the day. Well, he'd have to do better if he didn't want hurt feelings to ruin his plan.

"My ribs are a lot better, thanks. Since you, uh—" she shifted her knees away from him as she remembered his touch from the night before, "told me they were only bruised, I've hardly felt them." She tilted her head toward the orange mug on the steps. "I promise I don't keep my pet wasp in it. Go ahead before it gets cold. And my name's Doone, D-o-o-n-e," she concluded, as she continued to stare at the fiddle-head ferns that fountained out from beneath the steps.

D-o-o-n-e? Where did that come from? He braced a booted foot against the step and attempted to dismiss the question. He had no intention of filling his mind with useless details about her, he assured himself, as he leaned an elbow to his knee and took up the coffee. Besides, it was time to be the smooth operator and charm the pants off her. His elbow slipped dangerously close to the edge of his knee. He couldn't believe he'd thought that. Lowering his head, he took a sip of coffee concentrating on its rich aroma and the way it combined with the nutty smell of the split alder wood.

She really *had* made a decent cup, not the usual oil slick most people came up with when they worked with exotic blends. "Mmm, I see you found my Kenyan blend," he remarked after regaining his composure.

From only three feet away the sound of his baritone voice started a tingling sensation in her stomach that quickly found its way outward through each layer of her skin. She was blushing, she knew it! She had to get control of herself. This wasn't a chance encounter with Tom Selleck, and it wasn't a vacation, either, she reminded herself sharply. She was here with Mackenzie for only one thing, the Emerald Light Cafe. It was time to face him and get down to business. Was he coming back to Seattle with her or wasn't he? She set down her mug, laced her fingers together, and dutifully scooted to his side of the steps.

"Mackenzie," she began, turning to look at him. Both hands went halfway to her mouth and she held them there in a prayerlike position. "Mackenzie," she repeated in a rushing whisper, "you've shaved."

"And didn't nick myself once," he said, fingering his chin as he studied her lapis blue eyes less than a foot away.

"You look so different," she told him. Hunter watched, enchanted, as a grin spread over her face like the sunlight across the Sound earlier that morning. It felt as if the grin were embracing him in a friendly caress, and when she softened it to a smile, its warmth seeped through his bones and curled around his heart. Without taking his eyes from her he placed his mug on the deck. Why hadn't someone snatched her up? he wondered. And how could her eyes be so blue? He brushed a few wood chips from the side of his knee and leaned in toward her.

Doone realized immediately that he'd gotten rid of something else besides his beard and mustache. He'd gotten rid of the menacing facade and the frightening seriousness of last night. From the dimpled creases that bracketed his smile, to the sparkling warmth in his eyes, Hunter Mackenzie was now . . . approachable. Actually, approachable didn't begin to cover it. "You look so . . . different," she repeated. She watched, utterly fascinated, as the look in his soft gray eyes began revealing still another fact. He wanted her—as much as she wanted him.

He was so close Doone could smell him. A tempting blend of coffee, limes, and heated skin. "It's really me," she heard him say just before his mouth touched hers. His lips were warm and strong, and he knew how to use them. They hovered close to hers, barely touching her, constantly teasing her. Her eyelids drifted shut as she drank in the tender sensations. They flowed through her body drenching her senses relentlessly with a growing need for more. She shifted closer and slanted her mouth to feel the full impact of his lips on hers. He responded with a quick, hungry kiss, then pulled back. She opened her eyes and for what seemed like an eternity, watched him study her face. Then he kissed her again, a little longer this time. But not, she decided breathlessly, long enough.

Hunter shivered as he felt her warm hands skim his jawline. He could control his rising desire if he kept his hands off her body, he reasoned, and instead concentrated on delicately nibbling her lower lip. She tasted like heaven. Her fingertips were slipping past his ear lobes and down his neck. Then to his shoulders where she kneaded his muscles, causing a jealous throbbing elsewhere in his body. He grabbed for the edge of the step and leaned in closer. Her breath was coming faster, or was it his? He couldn't keep this up much longer. Then again, he quickly decided, if she stopped sliding those fingertips over the nape of his neck, he could maybe stand just a little more. She smelled like springtime and it had been a long, lonely winter. But if she kept up that throaty little moan, he swore he'd give in to the last vestige of his self-control. He'd tumble her to the carpet of wood chips and take her then and there.

Doone sensed his strained control and, forgetting everything else, instinctively wanted him to unleash it. Each time she touched him, each time she moved her fingertips along his skin more of his passion poured into their kiss and into her. She had, she realized, a lot to learn about kissing and he had so much to teach her; she could do this all day. And if his responses were any indication, so could Hunter Mackenzie. If he would just take her in his arms . . . She tasted his smooth shaven cheek, then sighed as his lips urged her mouth back to his. Her lips parted and he slid his tongue into the moist warmth beyond them. All day . . .

All day? God, she didn't have all day! Harry Shackley and the thousand dollars were waiting. And so was the unrealized dream of the Emerald Light Cafe. She had to stop this . . . in a moment. She urged one last exploration from his tongue, tasting the achingly sweet promise of what could have been. It was now or never. She pressed her hands against his chest and at the same time pulled back.

"We . . . h-have to . . . catch the . . . ferry," she whispered, noting her moistness on his mouth. His eyes changed from warm and drowsy to confused and then to freezing steel.

Hunter pushed himself up from the step and shook his head. She certainly had her priorities straight. She was still working for Shackley.

"We? What gave you that idea?" he asked, his

gaze locking with hers. With admirable control he brushed some nonexistent wood chips from the front of his shirt and picked up his mug. Acting as if the kiss had never happened, he took a quick sip of coffee and shrugged. "I never said I was going back."

She was on her feet and down the steps in an instant. "What? But—but you shaved," she said in disbelief at what was happening. She shoved a lock of curls behind one ear and held it there. "After you had a good night's sleep, I assumed—"

His reply contained a little more emotion than he would have liked. "Your assumption is incorrect, I had a lousy night's sleep."

"What is it with you? Why won't you go back to Seattle with me?" Her voice was steadily rising and she knew it and didn't care. She had more energy than she knew what to do with. "What's one day out of your life compared to my entire future?"

"I have plenty to do here without day tripping to Seattle," he said. He pitched out the remaining coffee and plunked the mug onto the deck. "Too much sugar," he explained sarcastically.

Doone nervously flicked her tongue over her lips and found the taste of him still lingering there. Damn him! She rubbed the back of her hand over her lips. How could she have let him kiss her like that? Well, she wasn't going to stick around and subject herself to a bunch of wayward hormones. She'd get the money together for the Emerald Light Cafe without his cooperation.

"You're a hermit. And you're not even an eccentric one, Mackenzie. You're just plain strange. Stay here working on your woodsman badge until next winter, if you like, but I'm not going to miss that ferry." She tugged the terry cloth tie tighter and slapped back a lock of hair. "Some people have schedules and deadlines, and I happen to be one of them."

Hunter Mackenzie sighed as he watched her take all three steps in one awkward leap. He'd known excitable women in his life, but this one took the cake. He dragged a hand down his face and swore he wasn't going to say another word. A walk would cool her down and then he would go after her and tell her as calmly as he could that she would have to put up with the "hermit" a little longer. He sat down on the edge of the deck, leaned back on one elbow and waited for her.

A few minutes later she reappeared in the doorway dressed in the tattered red gown. Clutched to her midriff was her evening bag and a pair of mud stained shoes. The final barrage began before she reached the steps.

"Thanks for your inimitable style of hospitality, Mackenzie." One shoe slipped from her grip and he picked it up before she had the chance.

"May I?" he asked, tossing the shoe in the air and catching it.

"You may not," she answered, snatching the shoe as he tossed it again. She was wearing what was probably his last clean pair of white wool socks and he winced as she went down the steps and out onto the wood chips.

Hesitating for a second, she turned back toward him. "Sometime, somewhere in your life, someone must have treated you poorly. But that's no reason to throw it back at me. Please," she said in an overly dramatic drawl, "don't attempt to get to me or pretend to apologize with those puppy dog eyes. Just listen to a little sense for a moment. If this is the way you treat your guests, you will fail as an innkeeper—as badly as you probably failed with Shackley."

Her ending remark brought him up from his elbows, onto his feet and across the soggy ground in one rushing motion. His fingers shook as he grabbed her shoulders. "Some people don't assume they know everything. They ask questions and wait for answers, Danielle, or whatever your name is. Some people appreciate a sane, cautious approach to life; they sort things—"

"Some people, Mr. Hunter Mackenzie, *do* get on with their lives," she shot back as she broke his grip with one flailing arm. "They do not mistake motion for movement. And my name is not Danielle!" she shouted before lifting the hem of her dress to carefully sidestep a water filled depression.

If he'd ever considered tearing his hair out it was now. A dozen retorts came to his tongue, but each one would, he knew, make him look like more of a fool in her eyes. And that was the last thing he wanted. In the end he watched his white wool socks slowly turn a muddy brown as she marched triumphantly across the clearing in them.

Doone moved on down the hill, silently castigating herself. She had done it again, opened her mouth and blown a probably reconcilable situation. If only she could get control of the tumultuous sensations that overtook her when he was near. When his dimples creased his cheeks, when he dragged a finger along his lip, when his eyes softened with a dimension of emotion she could only wonder at.

A small scream escaped her lips as Sheeba bounded out of the forest with a startling bark. When Doone had caught her breath, she brushed the prancing dog aside. "Go home, girl. Go on, go back. Shoo."

The delighted animal trotted beside her.

"Well, I don't blame you. Who'd want his company anyway?"

As if on cue, Sheeba spotted a movement in a thicket alongside the hill, howled as if in pain, and took off running.

Doone picked up the downhill pace as she spotted the rental car below. She had to get back to Seattle and call Ludlow & Associates. Cam *had* to have her property sold by now. And if he had, she would put the last twenty-four hours down to a bad and needless experience . . . well, most of it, she amended as her fingers moved along her lips.

Enough of that! It was time to blot Hunter Mackenzie from her mind and all the whirling emotions surrounding his image. She'd had the final word, she reminded herself. There should be some small triumph in that fact. But there wasn't. Only a terrible sense of loss. It was half the thousand dollars, of course. Or was it? She stopped her rapid descent of the hill and looked back. What was one day out of his life? He was as selfish as any man she'd ever known.

Reaching the rental car, Doone saw the rear tires were still hubcap deep in the mud. And without Hunter Mackenzie's assistance they would stay that way. She glanced up the hill. Absolutely not. She refused to even consider crawling back up to ask him for the favor. Besides, it was a beautiful morning. She'd walk to the ferry terminal. There was plenty of time and a lot of pent up energy from this morning's encounter with him. Doone examined one serviceable and one misshapened shoe and decided to try to save them to wear on the ferry. Chilly as they were, there was plenty of padding left in Mackenzie's socks.

Twenty minutes later she sank onto a sawed off tree trunk by the edge of the road. Just where was she? And why couldn't she feel her toes? She pushed off the mud soaked socks, pulled her feet onto the stump, and clamped both hands over her toes. Looking around the miniature rain forest of Eagle's Island, Doone drew in a deep breath. The fresh smell of balsam fir reminded her of Christmas. Christmas, she mused, looking back in the direction of Mackenzie's house. Maybe someday that wouldn't have such a melancholy ring to it, but right now she had other things to think about. The roads had looked considerably different from inside the car during last night's storm. Somewhere above her a busy woodpecker sounded. In just a moment she'd get her bearings and continue on, but right now she needed rest and a resupply of blood to her feet. With startling speed a ruby-throated hummingbird appeared in mid-air and nervously inspected a deep pink foxglove growing nearby. Doone rested her chin on her knees and sighed. Being alone out here didn't necessarily mean being lonely. Even as the sun slipped behind a cloud and it began to drizzle, her appreciation for Mackenzie's island grew.

But drizzle or no drizzle, she had to make that

morning ferry. The complicated winter ferry schedule still applied and she hadn't taken the time to find out if an evening ferry was scheduled for today. If she missed this morning's ferry, another twenty-four hours could pass before the next one docked or departed.

She tossed the socks aside and struggled into the high heeled shoes. Two yards down the road she heard an engine behind her. Looking over her shoulder, she saw Sheeba's glossy red head and neck straining out the window of Mackenzie's pickup truck. Before Doone could think what to do, he pulled the truck up alongside of her. He leaned his head out the window and adjusted the bill of his ball cap.

"Do you know where you're going, young lady?"

Doone cast a glance up and down the fir flanked road and then suspiciously toward Hunter. He was wearing a faded blue denim jacket with a turned up collar. His palm lay flat against the dark red door. He looked warm and dry and—that was enough of that! The question had almost formed on her lips, but instead of asking for the desperately needed answer, she turned and continued walking. No way would she ask him for a lift to town.

At the sound of Hunter's voice, Sheeba had begun to bark. The pickup glided along beside Doone as the dog wedged her head behind Hunter's with hysterical determination. The dog continued struggling to paw her way through the open window as she alternately whined and yowled with excitement.

Doone stopped just long enough to pull off her shoes. Barefoot, she quickened her pace.

"Doone, for God's sake, have you ever heard of hypothermia?"

Hypothermia? That was right below punctured lungs on her list of things to learn more about. And so what if he finally got her name right? It didn't mean a thing. She heard what sounded like the distinct grinding of gears behind her. That was it then. He was leaving her for good, and going home to his chopping block and blueprints. Doone took a shallow breath as she brushed the rain from her eyes with the back of her hand. When she opened them again, Hunter Mackenzie was standing before her.

"We have to talk," he said.

She squinted up at him through the quickening drizzle. "About what? I have to catch the ferry," she said, absently patting Sheeba's head as the dog leaned against her knee.

"I know you do. Doone, listen to me. You don't want to get yourself lost on these back roads. It could be a lot more dangerous than you think."

Doone eyed the surrounding forest. Hummingbirds and woodpeckers? Foxgloves and sunshine? Forcing back a smile, she stared diligently at his chin. "Wolves and bears, Mackenzie?"

Twin dimples creased his cheeks. "No. And no lions or tigers either. But I should warn you about the odor of wet dog. So, if you and Toto will get in the truck, we may be saved a very unpleasant smell. By the way," he said, taking off his jacket and placing it around her shoulders, "I don't hold out much hope for these ruby slippers." Taking them from her, he walked to the truck, opened the canopied back and tossed them in. He walked toward her and grinned. "Come on, you're beginning to look like a raccoon again."

"A bothersome one?" She smoothed two fingers under her eyes and then gave him a wry little smile.

His grip was warm and steady. "Not too, I hope," he said under his breath, as he helped her into the pickup.

"Did you say something?"

"No," he said, lifting her hem and tucking a spill of red silk into her hand.

Doone settled into the cab, enjoying the blast of heat coming from the vent near the floor. A ride to the village was exactly what she needed, and whether or not he boarded the ferry with her, didn't matter at the moment. She had begun to feel her toes again.

Hunter put a reluctant Sheeba into the canopied truck bed and pulled out a down vest before he closed the back of the truck. He slipped on the vest and climbed in behind the wheel.

"We seem to have gotten off on the wrong foot. First, I want to apologize for my inimitable style of hospitality. You were right, you didn't deserve to be treated like that." He hesitated, tipping the baseball cap up from his forehead. "I'm sorry if I frightened or offended you in any way." He placed a half opened California poppy on the dashboard in front of her. "They came early this year," he said, nodding toward the blossom.

She picked up the blossom and twirled it between her fingertips. Frightened her? Offended her? Her mind filled with the memory of his kiss and the interior of her mouth began to tingle. She swallowed. "I'm the one who needs to make an apology. I don't know what got into me, losing my temper like that. Thank you for coming, and for this," she said lifting the peace offering in his direction.

Hunter watched her close her eyes and bury her nose in the egg yolk colored flower. She was near enough for him to gather her into his arms and have her bother him again. He felt his throat constrict and turned his gaze toward the windshield. Thrusting the truck into gear, he proceeded to make a tight U-turn in the road.

"This place is incredibly beautiful. How did you come to choose it for your home and the inn?"

"My family's from the area, so I spent most of my summers on this island as a child. I'd planned to come straight back here from military service but Harry Shackley got to me first with an offer to save the world from more bad guys. That kept me away from here for more than a decade."

Doone noticed his hands sliding to the top of the steering wheel until all eight fingers pressed together. Harry Shackley again. She forced a carefree tone into her voice. "It's quite a walk to the village, isn't it?"

He turned onto a side road. "That it is."

"Except for my feet, I kind of enjoyed it, though. I saw the most incredible hummingbird. I could practically touch it." She caught sight of two peeling madrona trees whizzing by the window and twisted her head as far as she could until she lost sight of them. "Thanks again for coming after me, I must have been lost. I could have sworn I passed those very trees a few minutes ago."

Hunter said nothing. He switched on the radio and turned the knob until he'd come to a station playing early Beatles' music. She'd be finding out soon enough that he wasn't taking her to the village. He looked over and saw her patting her knees to the beat of the music.

A few minutes later, she pressed her palms against the dashboard and peered through the windshield. "Mackenzie, that's my rental car, and that's . . . your house up there." She turned to him, giving him a puzzled, disappointed look. "Why did you bring me back here?"

The truck's four wheel drive made the steep incline in less than a minute. Hunter turned off the ignition, lifted his cap, and scratched his head. This wasn't going to be easy.

"Mackenzie, I'm going to be late for the ferry."

Hunter twisted in his seat, resting his back against the door. The Beatles were wailing out "All My Lovin'," and Doone had just folded her arms across her chest like a squatting cossack. He couldn't help himself, he had to smile. The longer he looked at her, the longer he wanted to. She was bright and beautiful and funny. And how he wanted to kiss those tiny ears of hers and . . . more. But this wasn't getting the job done.

His voice was suddenly serious. "I can't let you take that ferry this morning."

She looked across the cab and met his stare head on. "What exactly does that mean? You sound like I'm a hostage or something."

Hunter's stare drifted up toward the ceiling. "I have to sort through the documents you brought me," he lied, as he pictured himself burning everything in the fireplace the night before. He had started spinning a concentric web of lies that took them further and further from the truth. In fact, he'd just trapped her with a lie. And he'd keep her here with more, if he had to.

She studied him closely. After his kisses, after his apology, she knew he wouldn't actually hurt her. But waiting until this moment to tell her he didn't want her leaving was a bit unsettling. What was in those damn documents anyway to make him behave like this? "Can't you read them on the ferry ride back to Seattle?"

He shook his head. "They need very thorough studying. Besides, you said you were interested in the full thousand dollar payment."

A relieved smile spread across her face. "So you're saying you'll go back as soon as you've finished reading what I brought from Mr. Shackley."

"I'm not promising that," he said quietly.

Doone wriggled her finger into the hole in her sleeve and attempted to pull the edges together. He was so right about the money. She needed all of it, but possibly getting fired from the hostessing job at Firebird's was more than she wanted to gamble. Damn him! She looked out the window beside her and tried unsuccessfully to control the anger in her voice. "If I decided to go along with this, exactly how long would your sorting through take? I've got a schedule that's screaming for attention."

"A while," he hedged, shoving his fingers again through the thick curly waves near his temple.

She threw the flower onto the dashboard. Turning to face him, she braced one arm on the dashboard and one on the back of the seat. "How long, Mackenzie? I need to know."

His gaze traced her riotous curls, the slender column of her neck, and all the treasures of her face. The pursed lips, the pert nose, and those brilliant lapis eyes. The armor he'd worn so long began dropping away.

"As long as I need you."

FOUR

Hunter stared across the truck's interior at Doone's rigid profile. So proud, so defiant. And so trapped. He scratched his eyebrow with the back of his thumb and began to feel trapped himself. Trapped in the reprehensible situation he'd created. She hadn't bargained for captivity when she'd agreed to come out here. She deserved an explanation. His shoulders drooped for an instant and he closed his eyes. Or maybe he needed to talk.

Needed to talk? Hadn't he told himself Doone Daniels wasn't going to change anything? Especially that frozen moment of hell lodged in his soul? He heard her huffy little sigh and looked up. She'd lifted her chin higher, unknowingly emphasizing the delicate cords at the base of her throat. In her efforts to remain aloof and, therefore, in control, she'd managed to offer him palpable evidence of her flesh and blood spirit. That spirit pulsed strong in the graceful curve of her throat. Something wonderful caught, then twisted inside him. Life. She pulsed with life.

He blinked and felt something ease within his chest. Recognizing it in her had caused a surge of replenishment within himself.

He blinked again and the words slipped out effortlessly. "I don't know what Shackley told you, but I worked in Portugal a number of years before coming back to Washington State. I've been trying to put . . . that time in Portugal behind me," he said quietly. "With what you brought me, I've got to decide whether to return there or not. I'm really sorry for any inconvenience this will cause you, but Shackley is asking for a slice of me. I'm not about to hand it to him like birthday cake. I have to have time to think it over." He watched her eyelids flicker, but that chin never moved. "With you here, Shackley will ease off, he won't be on my back trying to tip the scales." He waited a while longer for her to respond. When she didn't, the renewed and recognizable flow within him pulsed a little slower. If she would only talk to him. . . . He closed his eyes and for the briefest moment experienced a strange emptiness where that frozen hell had been.

There was more he wanted to say. So much more. *With you here I don't feel like Christina's gravestone.* He sighed and got out of the truck.

If he did return to Portugal, he'd have no trouble resuming his cover. He hadn't forgotten how to tell a half-truth or how to deceive an innocent for the sake of the operation. He thought about the two fishermen he'd chosen to pose as smugglers that night a year ago. Neither he nor his fishermen had anticipated a surprise entrance from Christina nor the subsequent explosion of gunfire. Their steadfastness that night had astonished him. Waiting until Christina's killer, Luis, and his two men had fled, the fishermen had dragged him and Christina's body back to their boat.

Putting their lives or the lives of others in similar jeopardy again was something he didn't want to think about. Especially since, according to the documents Doone had brought him, Luis now traveled with as many as five well armed men—enough to wipe out a score of staunchly loyal fishermen.

He walked to the rear of the truck, lifted the hatch back and released the straining Irish setter. "Let those chipmunks be," Hunter shouted as the dog hit the ground running.

He knew he wasn't playing fair with Doone. She also had a life to live. Guilty or not, his spirits were already lifting as he walked to the cab's window and glanced in. That chin was as high as ever and that nose was, too. He smiled at her stubbornness. Who had he been kidding? He didn't want her to leave for more reasons than he'd admitted, both to himself and to her. He didn't want her to leave until he'd brought that chin down a notch. Not until he'd heard her laugh again. Not until he'd tasted her mouth and felt its unrestrained response again. The memory of that sweet, eager mouth of hers sent a thrill through him. He tossed his keys in the air before pocketing them in his down vest.

Doone watched him saunter across the clearing and up the stairs of the deck. Was he whistling?! How could he seem to be so caring one minute and so damn selfish the next? And what about Portugal? Why hadn't he explained more about Portugal? She hadn't tried to stop him from telling her more, he'd stopped himself. She'd been straight with Hunter Mackenzie all along, but things were going to change! She counted slowly to ten, then stepped out of the truck and slammed the door with enough enthusiasm to rattle both its windows.

She recaptured a handful of her dress and stalked into the house and then the kitchen. He wasn't there, but his vest was. His vest with the keys?! She tiptoed to the kitchen door, pressed her back against the wall and stuck her head back into the living room. She breathed a sigh of relief. He wasn't in the living room. Dashing back across the kitchen to the vest, she rapidly searched every pocket. The keys weren't there. She shook and patted the entire garment, then threw it to the table as she scanned the counter tops and the table. Those keys had to be here someplace. She shoved back her hair with both hands. What could he have done with them? Dropping to her knees, she began a frantic search under the table.

"Looking for these?" came a voice from behind her.

Startled, she lifted her head, banging it hard on the table's edge.

He was down on his haunches before she could finish her expletive rich reaction. "My, my, my. Such language. That last one even made me blush."

"Damn you, Mackenzie, I want to go home. And don't you dare tell me to click my ruby heels together or I'll strangle you," she shouted, scrambling to her feet and rubbing her head. She stared at the ring of keys dangling from his fingertips.

Hunter reached out and pressed the keys into her

hand. His fingers instinctively curled around the coolness of hers. Without thinking, he brought his other hand under the tangle of their fingers and lifted them to his lips. Slowly he opened his hand, turned hers over, and blew on it to warm her. "Sweetheart, you're freezing."

Doone watched his coppery tipped eyelashes descending as he lowered his mouth to her hand. If she allowed his lips to touch her skin, she knew she might abandon every shred of reason for wanting to leave, and she couldn't do that. She pulled back her hand, but not before his lips had grazed it.

"I'm . . . fine. Thank you," she whispered, pressing the keys along with the sensation of his lips to her chest. She watched as he straightened up. By the calm way he studied her, it was obvious who had the better control.

"Not that they'll do you much good. While you were playing hide and seek under the table, I was on the phone. The ferry terminal was damaged during last night's storm. Until it's fixed, you're stuck here anyway."

She stared mutely at the keys, then at him. "You're making this up," she said slowly, doubt clouding her eyes.

Hunter rubbed the back of his neck and thought about another strand in his web of deceit. "No, I'm not. I called—"

"On what, Mackenzie? A string and two tin cans?" Spunkiness returned to her voice as she cut him off. "I 'reconnoitered' this place last night, just in case you've forgotten. I didn't see a telephone."

Hunter smiled. Such righteous indignation. "I keep it in a drawer in my bedroom."

"You what?"

"If I want to talk with someone I plug it in. Otherwise, I've no use for the damn thing," he explained, as he watched the tiny wrinkle appear between her brows again. "I know what you're thinking. But forget about using it, the phone went dead before I could finish the call. It's usually out of service a few days when it goes dead like that." He watched her fold her arms across her midriff and shake her head. "What's the matter, don't you believe me?"

She narrowed her eyes and lowered her chin. "Not as far as I can throw you, and I'd say I couldn't even lift you up to try."

Hunter laughed at the image of such a thing, and at the same time watched her press the keys against her mouth, and turn her head. She managed to hide her smile, but failed to maintain the stubborn straightness in her shoulders. They heaved slightly before she took a deep breath and faced him again. He pulled a chair between them and straddled it. Minutes passed. Indecision cloaked her eyes each time she looked at him. He'd have to go for the big bluff or lose her.

"Anyway," he said casually, "I've gotten some clothes together for you. They're in the empty room next to mine." He rested his chin on the back of the chair and smiled. "I really like you in dripping red silk," he said, playfully lifting his eyebrows, "but I know the ticket seller in Evergreen Village, and I'd never hear the end of it, especially since you'll have to drive back here in my truck to spend the night."

He stood up, replaced the chair and left her in the kitchen holding the keys.

He must be telling her the truth. Why else would he trust her with the truck keys? And what clothes of his, she wondered with a shake of her head, had he picked out for her?

A few minutes later Doone was looking at a ladies' red cashmere sweater and a pair of fine wool, black gaucho pants resting on a gaily painted, probably Portuguese, chair. Her first reaction was to stroke the soft, inviting materials and marvel at the designer quality of each item of clothing. The labels, she quickly noted, weren't in English, and it was obvious the clothing had never been worn before.

She held both items up against her body and looked down. They were going to fit her perfectly. Frowning, she lowered the garments. Why did he have these here? Who was suppose to be wearing them? And why was she suddenly so apprehensive about putting them on? Replacing the clothes on the chair, she picked up the discarded tissue paper and slowly crumpled it.

If he'd wanted her to know, he would have told her. And she wasn't going to ask. Because if she did ask, it would prove to him that she had more than a casual curiosity concerning him. Then he would continue with those looks, those smiles, those touches. She flung the tissue paper to the floor.

She *did* have more than a casual curiosity concerning Hunter Mackenzie, though, and she had to fight it. No matter how strong the desire, giving in to a moment of passion with him while knowing he could be flying off to Portugal tomorrow didn't make sense. At least, not within her realm of experience. This pull between them had to be ignored, for the sake of her future. For the dream she'd put off long enough. She wasn't going to stray from her objective a moment longer. The Emerald Light Cafe needed money and *he* was just the instrument she needed to get it. The time remaining with Mackenzie would be spent on the business of convincing him to return to Seattle with her. Doone changed into the new clothes, picked up her evening bag and, barefoot, headed back to Mackenzie.

He rose from the sofa, an oblong box in his hands, and watched her pirouette across the living room. She flipped the ends of her hair around her shoulders. "I probably need a classic Spanish hairdo to go with the gaucho pants, but I don't have my styling mousse with me." She ran her hands down the sleeves of the thigh length sweater. "Good fit," she concluded, then looked down and wriggled her toes.

Hunter had watched her twirl around and in that moment experienced more conflicting emotions than he'd ever imagined possible. Those were definitely Christina's clothes, but she would have never moved in them with such uncontrived grace. Christina would have had her hair sleeked back, not tumbling wantonly around her face and shoulders. There would have been a jangling of solid gold bracelets at Christina's wrists and large, perfectly formed loops hanging from her ears, not the pearls he'd just glimpsed. Alarmed at how easily he recalled those details, he lowered his gaze. Barefoot! Christina would never leave her dressing area, let alone their villa until she was completely ready. He shifted the box in his hands as he recalled Christina's nightly ritual. She would send the maid down to announce her. He'd be pacing in the foyer, wondering if this would finally be the time she was late. At the last possible moment, and already laughing at his impatience, Christina would appear at the head of the stairs. No matter where they might be headed, her comment was always the same. "But, darling, they wouldn't dare start without us." He winced at the striking clarity of the remembered scene.

"Mackenzie? Yoo hoo? I said you don't need to worry, I'll be very careful with these. I can see they're quite expensive," Doone repeated, wondering what thoughts had clouded those nickel gray eyes.

Hunter blinked. He looked at her fresh face not ten feet from his own, at the light dusting of freckles on her nose, and the curious gleam in her bright blue eyes. He reached up and rubbed his brows. Expensive? He'd be paying for Christina the rest of his life.

Don't, Doone wanted to say. Don't think about her, whoever she is. Think about me! But then she recalled the conclusion she'd just reached and the promise she'd made to herself. *Keep him out of your heart, but get him on your side*. She opened her evening bag and brought out two sets of keys. "Mackenzie!"

He lifted his hand away from his brow and looked up.

"Catch!"

Instinctively his hand shot to the left across his body and closed around the two sets of keys.

"I won't need your truck, Mackenzie, but when it's time to go, I'll need my car out of that ditch."

After slipping the keys into his pocket, he opened the box. "Hopefully these will fit. Then you can have a look at what keeps me here and not with Shackley. The inn, or at least what's completed."

"And if the boots don't fit, I make myself content with the blueprints, right?" she said, pulling out a pair of black suede boots. She sat down in the rocking chair and began tugging one on.

"Hell, no," he announced with mock severity. "If they don't fit, I'll just throw you over my shoulder and carry you over there."

"You wouldn't dare," she said, deciding in that instant that no matter how badly the boots might fit, she wouldn't admit it. What he'd made sound like a comical scene could become too intimate to withstand her new resolve. The boots did pinch. "Perfect," she lied.

She followed him out of the house and across the deck. Again, she was struck by the incredible beauty of the island Hunter Mackenzie had chosen to live on. The rain had stopped, but evidence of the drizzle dripped from every bush and tree surrounding them. Who else, she wondered, came to visit him here? Where was his family? His friends? But she shouldn't be asking these questions! The less she knew about him, the easier it would be to leave when the time came.

After a long walk along a path lined with blackberry canes and waxy leaved shrubs and through a stand of old growth firs, Mackenzie led her near the back of a long, two story structure built on the side of the hill.

"It's not finished," Hunter explained, with a mixture of pride and defensiveness. What he'd accomplished was impressive and he knew it, but the inn should have been completed and in operation long before now. That fact had never bothered him until this moment.

"It smells new," Doone said, inhaling the cedar fragrance coming from the yellowish shakes covering the outside of the building. She reached out to touch the factory label stuck to one of the windows. "And I'm so jealous I could spit. Do you know how fortunate you are to be able to touch your dream, Mackenzie?" She looked up at him and smiled. Someday soon she hoped she'd be experiencing the same feelings as he when she refurbished the loft for the Emerald Light Cafe. She sighed. It might not be in her best interest to think so, but Mackenzie had a handsome handful to contend with right here. He didn't need Harry Shackley bothering him.

He gave the back of his neck a light scrubbing with his knuckles and shrugged. "I'd be interested in what you have to say once you've seen the place. Word's getting around the area about it, but I haven't let many people get a peek. It's coming together piecemeal because I'm doing most of it by myself."

She looked first at the building, then a stack of lumber and finally an upturned wheelbarrow before returning her gaze to him. "But it's such a big project. You mean you don't have a partner?"

His entire manner suddenly changed. His eyes

took on the dark, flat color of the sound before a storm. "I don't need a partner."

She couldn't have been more certain she'd said the wrong thing if he'd held her down and washed out her mouth with soap. There had to be some way to recapture the easy level they'd gotten themselves to only a moment ago. "I understand," she managed casually. Then the words came to her. "I know exactly what you mean."

"You do?" he asked suspiciously.

She made a concentrated effort to look interested in the small tear she'd made in the paper window label. She slipped the edge of her thumb nail under the corner and scraped. "Hmmm? Oh, of course. Partners have a way of complicating matters, slowing progress, draining a person's energies all at the same time." Brushing the flecks of paper from her fingers, she started down the side steps attached to the large building. "Unless they're family. By the way, you're going to need a razor blade to remove those labels."

Hunter watched her for a moment, then followed her down the steps. Just when he thought he had her pegged, she revealed another surprising facet. He almost bumped into her when she stopped short of the deck which ran across the front of the building. She was staring, speechless, across the circular drive.

"Beautiful," she murmured.

"I thinned out the trees last week. The two hundred foot vantage point above Puget Sound is suppose to catch your attention. I guess it works. You can see the . . . other islands," he managed to conclude as he noticed the huge object moving into view. The ferryboat was gliding into the sylvan studded seascape he'd created, and if she saw it, all hell would break loose. He stepped down beside her, pulled her onto the deck and positioned her against the wall.

"Well," she began breathlessly, looking up into his face, "I would have moved eventually."

"I, uh, just wanted to have your attention . . ." he began, not knowing what he was going to say next. Having her so close, he almost didn't care. Then he remembered the ferry and his remarks about it not coming. She'd be furious if she knew it was docking soon.

"You have my attention," she said, "but I wasn't finished looking at that magnificent view, if you don't mind." Actually, the view of Hunter Mackenzie was magnificent but, close as he was, too tempting. And she'd already decided to avoid that temptation. She started moving to one side, but he blocked her by placing both his hands on the wall next to her shoulders.

"Is this where you attach a ball and chain, or are you protecting me from one of those furry creatures again?" she asked, her body tensing as he drew closer.

"I need your . . . opinion about something," he said, his voice lowering to an involuntary whisper. He took a deep breath and reminded himself that the main objective to cornering her was to block her view. But she was so desirable, and so close . . .

"My opinion?" Pressing her palms to the wall alongside her hips, she licked warily at the corner of her mouth. Despite the mid-morning breeze, she was feeling decidedly warm right through to her muscles.

He moved his head a little closer. "Flowers."

"Flowers?" she repeated. Then, more softly, "What about flowers?" Glancing at his tanned, muscular arms penning her against the wall, she remembered how close those arms had come to holding her this morning when he'd kissed her. Those strong arms were now so close she could lean her cheek against their sinewy cords for some badly needed support. But shaking knees or not, she couldn't do that. With a sharp intake of air, she attempted to chase the thought, shifting her gaze toward the half-barrels stacked along the deck.

"For the front entrance of the inn. There, on the deck," Hunter explained, his gaze roaming her face and the thick volume of curls surrounding it. Once he started looking at her, it was hard to stop . . . but, he quickly rationalized, it didn't matter if being this close blocked her view of the ferry. As her curls lifted in the light breeze, he captured a shiny one between his fingers and toyed with the silky strands. He hadn't felt so high since climbing that switch back trail near Hurricane Ridge last month. His gaze drifted down to a pair of drowsy blue eyes and he knew by the stirrings within himself that dealing with her closeness was quite a different kind of challenge.

"Uh, petunias work quite well." As his face came closer she swallowed and pressed her head against the cedar shakes. "Yes, petunias," she repeated quickly, lifting her chin and meeting his look head-on. She felt her jaws growing weaker. He had the most compelling masculine presence she'd ever experienced. She opened her mouth to speak, but nothing came out. In fact, the very words left her head. Closing her eyes in utter frustration over losing the thought, she found herself asking the only question that really mattered. Why couldn't she just enjoy him as he seemed to be enjoying her? She felt her heart and mind pulling in two different directions as she fought for an answer. But the answer didn't come.

Having her near enough to hold made his body ache to do just that. Hunter eased closer, inserting his knee between hers with the determined grace of a lover. "And what else?" he whispered, stroking her cheek with his thumb.

"Trailing . . . red . . . geraniums," she managed as he took her jaw within his calloused fingertips. His lips brushed hers. Delicate explosions of pleasure were rocketing through her body, breaking down the last vestiges of defensive reasoning. He lowered his hand, encircling her breast, then capturing it with whisper-soft pressure. His weapon was tenderness, his assault, total, and she knew he was winning.

"Any more suggestions?" he asked, his voice husky. When she didn't respond, he feathered his fingers over her breast until his thumb found the pebbly peak of her nipple. "Tell me what else I need," he demanded in a barely audible whisper, his pulse pounding in his ears. If he kissed her long enough and deep enough, he reasoned, she'd be sure to close her eyes and then an entire fleet of ferries could motor past unseen. It would have to be some kiss, he thought, watching her eyes widen and a soundless gasp form on her lips as his hand trailed down her stomach to her hip.

"Marigolds, lots and lots of marigolds." Her own voice sounded far away. She looked up and for a timeless moment slipped, warm and trembling, into the relentless caress of his gaze. His hand slipped back to her breast and the world began dissolving into an ocean of molten nickel.

"Marigolds," he whispered, his lips hovering near hers. His senses were filled with her and yet he wanted more. "Where can I get marigolds?"

"The Public Market . . . Seattle. I could . . . help you." She moistened her lips and swallowed again. His nearness alone overwhelmed her senses, promising her paradise. She wanted to capture that promise and hold it close . . . forever. But promises had been broken before.

He leaned in close to her ear. "When?" he demanded in a whisper just before his lips brushed her ear. When was she going to realize how much he wanted her and how much she wanted him?

"Saturday," she whispered back, her voice cracking. She twisted away from the rivering warmth of his tongue in a half-hearted attempt to stop him. Undaunted, he nuzzled past her ear, pressing a trail of kisses that effectively blotted out the last of her frantic reasoning. She reached to his sides and curled her fingers over his belt. She didn't want to think any more, only to *be*.

He had told himself she had to want this, too. When she began tugging insistently at his belt, he took it for the proof he'd been waiting for. He gave in to the explicit invitation, pressing the evidence of his arousal against her. "Saturday? Who knows where we'll be Saturday?" Hunter said in a ragged whisper. And who cared? The world could end tonight and he'd already be in heaven. She tilted her hips against the rigidness between them and a frantic little moan escaped her throat. The sound echoed through every cell of his manhood heightening his hunger for her. He swore under his breath in disbelief at just how ready he was, then quickly gathered her into his arms. He slanted his mouth over hers and drank in the trembling sensations of her lips. He urged them apart, slipping his tongue along their silky moistness. He wanted a fuller embrace and, as if she'd read his mind, she ran her hands around his waist and pressed them into the small of his back.

Doone felt his muscles shivering under her touch. She continued touching, pressing, stroking him with a new urgency. Desire to have him closer sent her swaying in his arms. God, who knew where they'd be Saturday? Who cared? This moment was more than magical, it was real. And it was now. But the first doubts began to form as his last words played through her mind again and again. Who knew where . . . he'd be on Saturday? Here in her arms? Or Portugal?

"Where?" she managed breathlessly between their skirmishing kisses.

"Anywhere," Hunter answered, raising his head and smiling. He'd make love with her anywhere she wanted. He cupped her face in his hands and drank in her gaze. The fragile light shimmering deep in her eyes made him ache to please her.

"Portugal?" she asked, a tone of apprehension creeping into her voice.

"Portugal?" he echoed.

"Will you be in Portugal, or will you be here on Saturday?"

He came to earth with a crash. Of course, how could he have forgotten? She had come here for a purpose and while he had momentarily forgotten it, she certainly hadn't. He held his breath, then exhaled slowly. He rested his forehead against hers, feeling each deep breath she was fighting for. And then he understood. Her need for self-protection was as great as his own, and despite the throbbing ache in his groin, he was almost glad she'd brought up Portugal. Almost. She wouldn't be just a walk through the clover and neither of them needed the serious complication of beginning a relationship just now.

"Doone, Doone, Doone," he whispered, still treasuring the feel of her in his arms. A woman like this needed something more than erotic release and right now he couldn't promise anything else.

He sighed and gently pushed away from her as he turned to face the Sound. The ferry was out of sight. At least he'd solved that problem.

He propped his foot up on a stack of barrel halves and looked out beyond the cliff. Far in the distance a sailboat skimmed the surface, its white sails filled to stiffness.

"It's an honest question, and you deserve an honest answer. But, I can't tell you I'll be here when I don't know myself."

He rubbed his face, trying to think of something better to say. Nothing came. He looked back over his shoulder, but she turned her head and was stroking her brow, obviously to avoid looking at him. The least he could do would be to allow her some privacy. "I, uh, think I'll go and dig your car out of the mud," he said, stepping from the deck.

Doone watched him pick up a shovel from a pile of tools and cross the front yard before he disappeared through the tree-lined drive entrance. She slammed her fist back against the wall. She'd been a fool to allow him so close. Anger welled inside of her. Anger at herself for taking such a risk with him. She didn't need to know how much she could want him, damn it! She shoved her hair behind her ears and fought to get control of her breathing. Like the others, he could leave and never return to share the dreams. Hadn't she vowed never to hurt again? With each remembered sorrow a little sting returned, but this fresh hurt had a piercing strength all its own.

She ran back up the stairs, through the trees, and then along the path to the house. There had to be a way off this island, she told herself as she went into Mackenzie's bedroom and slammed the door. She'd never felt so trapped, but she couldn't stay in his bedroom avoiding him indefinitely. She rushed over to the nightstand beside the bed and yanked open the drawer. The phone was exactly where he said it was. "Please work!" she whispered desperately, unwinding the cord and plugging it into the phone jack. The dial tone sounded loud and strong. She punched out the number to Shackley's office and then hugged the receiver to her ear praying for him to answer. If he had to send a seaplane for her, he was going to get her off this island and away from Mackenzie.

"Hello, Mr. Shackley. Yes, it's me," she began. And then, "Well, he hasn't decided what he's going to do, but that's not—"

Before she could complete the sentence, Mackenzie whipped the phone out of her hands. Glaring at her, he brought the receiver to his ear. "Goodbye, Harry!" he said, without breaking his stare with her. With a quick and violent jerk he ripped the wire from the phone jack, shattering the small piece of plastic at its end. A chunk of mud fell from the back of his hand as he dropped the phone to the floor.

"Were you that impatient to tell him what was happening out here?" he asked, his eyes hard as steel. "Is that why you had to know if I was going back to Portugal? Is it?" he demanded, his words scraping at her heart.

Doone stood rooted to the floor, unable to utter a word. He took a step forward, then stopped short. A wall of ice had formed between them, shutting him off from her. She felt the waves of coldness emanating from it with each of his words. "I don't like being used like that." She had never seen anger like this before.

"Get your things together. The ferry passed the southeast tip five minutes ago and should be docking at Evergreen Village any time now." He threw her car keys into her hands. "If you hurry, you can make it back to Shackley today with a full report."

FIVE

Doone shoved open the door to Harry Shackley's office. She found him sitting behind his desk admiring the rich gleam of the elegant leather shoe he held in his hand.

"Pretty ticked, was he?" he asked, not bothering to look up. He dabbed more dark paste onto the instep. The ever-present, unlit cigar moved between his lips as he resumed his buffing.

She walked in and slammed the door. "You're disgusting." She watched as Shackley tossed the stained cloth to the floor and inserted a hand into each one. He held them up to catch the light from a nearby window.

Winking, he twisted the shoes in her direction. "What do you think?"

"They're too good for you, but that's beside the point." Striding to the window she yanked the cord and the blinds clattered closed. "I have no intention of sharing the spotlight with a pair of shoes when I ask you this."

Shackley smiled, slipped the shoes into their individual flannel drawstring storage bags and carefully placed them in the bottom drawer of his desk. "So, what's up?"

"What happened to him last year in Portugal?"

Harry Shackley studied her for a moment, then rested his head against the back of his chair. His voice was a mixture of indulgence and impatience. "I take it you didn't get an answer from him about that."

"Not enough of one," she snapped, walking over to the coffee machine. She stared at dried coffee splatters on the top of the file cabinet. Pushing back the sleeves of the borrowed cashmere sweater, she was reminded once again that she hadn't gotten around to finding out a lot of things that she desperately wanted to know.

Closing her eyes, she recalled the last moments with Mackenzie. There was no way she could defend the phone call to Harry Shackley while looking into Mackenzie's steel-cold eyes. Mackenzie had been in such an agitated state by then that dropping to her knees and begging him to see her side of it wouldn't have changed his mind. The first light of trust that had begun to glow in those magical eyes of his had been snuffed out by the time he'd ripped the phone from her hands. She'd shivered then, not from fright, but from the look in his eyes of a person betrayed.

There was more to remember from her short visit than that horrific moment when he'd sent her away, though. She'd witnessed glimpses of the man he had been and she couldn't ignore the unanswered questions raised by those glimpses. She ached to know more about the passions that ruled him. There was a dark justification for what tormented him, and she had to hear it before going on with her own life and the plans for the Emerald Light Cafe. The golden images of his laughter, his kisses, his questioning looks kept flashing through her mind, demanding the entire story. And Harry Shackley was going to tell it to her. On the ferry back from Eagle's Island, she'd figured out a way to insure that. She poured a cup of coffee and turned around.

"I'll take a cup," he said.

"Go ahead and get it. I don't work for you any more." She watched his eyes narrow for an instant. Then the familiar shark-like grin returned. That's right, she thought, get a bit suspicious. I mean business.

"All right, you got the dirty end of the stick," he admitted, "but for the money I offered, it wasn't so bad. I know Mac and he'd never hit a woman." He lifted his feet, resting them on his desk. "It was a lot better than sitting around an old man's office straightening magazines—" he began as he stretched out his arms, then cradled the back of his head in his hands.

"You're not listening." But he would be when he realized that the girl scout he'd sent out had come back a storm trooper. "What really happened to him? And don't tell me it's secret agent burn out, or so help me, I'll pour this coffee right in your lap." She took a step toward the desk.

The gamble began to pay off. Both of Shackley's hands shot out from behind his head. "Whoa, whoa, whoa. Calm down."

"One more time, Shackley. This is as calm as I'm going to get today." She plunked the Styrofoam cup on his desk. "Try this one. Whose clothes am I wearing?"

"I know you think you deserve some answers, but there's no way I can explain this. You don't have the clearances. And even if you did, you wouldn't have an official need to know anyway." He lifted his rump and repositioned it in the chair. "Hey," he began, as she reached for the telephone on his desk. "What are you doing? Who are you—?" His feet hit the floor as she punched out three numbers.

"Hello, police?"

"Are you crazy?!" Aided by the spring action of the chair, he lunged over the desk toward her. "Hang up!"

Doone placed her hand over the mouth piece and pulled the telephone from his reach. "I have the telephone number of the Seattle *Times* in my bag. I'm sure some investigative reporter would love to know about this—what do you people call this place?—the cover office."

He hesitated a moment, then dropped his gaze and nodded reluctantly. Doone replaced the receiver and sat down. "To answer your question, no, I am not crazy. I am hurt, I am humiliated, and most of all, I am very angry." Harry Shackley didn't have to know about the guilt she felt, and he didn't have to know about the new and empty aching spot inside her now that Hunter Mackenzie couldn't stand the sight of her. "So explain to me why he's pulled out of the land of the living."

"What exactly has he told you?"

Doone related the sketchy facts Mackenzie had supplied. Shackley nodded, pulled the cigar from his mouth and rubbed his nose. When he finally spoke his voice was dry and serious. "I'll tell you what I can, but if it goes any further than this room, you're taking a chance on some good people's lives."

She nodded.

He waited a moment, then nodded back and stood beside the desk. He picked up her coffee cup and drank from it. Nervously patting the back of his thin, gray hair he turned and walked over to the window. Lifting a blind, he peered out into the Seattle sunshine.

A strange calm had settled over her. It didn't matter if Shackley took all day to explain, just knowing the information was forthcoming had soothed her considerably. She poured herself another cup of coffee.

"Mac had the smoothest undercover operation I'd ever been involved with. He ostensibly managed a hotel's casino in the Algarve, that's the southern coastal region of Portugal. We were just about to catch one of the biggest and nastiest drug smugglers ever targeted." Shackley let the end of the blind pling into place before he turned to face her. "Things, uh, got out of hand and Mac's partner was shot and killed. He has some fool notion it was his fault."

"His partner?" Doone asked, suddenly fidgety within the borrowed sweater.

Shackley wiped the perspiration from the side of his nose, then glanced at his fingers. "After it happened I went to the villa myself, packed up her things and sent them to her sister. Those clothes you're wearing were delivered the day after, so I put them in with Mac's and sent them out here," he explained, looking her over. "Always the best for her. She was a beauty. That classical Latin look, but with the savvy of a street fighter. I hand-picked her myself," he said, shaking his head with a secret smile. "She and Mac were the best pair in the field . . . but in the end, she let personal things get in the way." He pulled the cord, raising the blinds and letting in the light. "Anyway, she's gone. No one can bring her back, and we still have this slime out there who's setting up another network. Before it gets out of hand, I want Mac back in place where he belongs."

Mackenzie hadn't been licking his wounded pride, he'd been trying to deal with the death of a partner . . . or was she more than a fellow employee? What had Shackley said? . . . "a beauty . . . she and Mac . . . personal reasons." *Personal reasons*. Doone sat down and stared into the palms of her hands. Personal reasons—like loving each other? Why else would Mackenzie behave the way he did. The woman he'd loved had been murdered and, as if that weren't bad enough, he felt responsible. And Shackley wanted him to go back, to pick up where he'd left off, to put aside pain that hadn't finished hurting.

The borrowed black suede boots were burning blisters against her heels. "But he's not ready. Get someone else. No one is irreplaceable, Shackley."

Shackley studied her as he swallowed the last of the coffee. "You didn't get to know Mac as well as I thought you would. There's no one like him. He's coming back, honey. And the sooner, the better. Whether or not you help me with him.''

Jumping to her feet, her fists were clenched at her waist. "For God's sake, can't you see he's hurting? Don't you know what it feels like when people you love die?!''

"This line of questioning isn't just on humanitarian grounds, is it? It's on a more personal level now, I see.''

She shot him a warning look.

"I thought so,'' he concluded smugly.

Dropping her fists, Doone looked away from his uncompromising stare. At this point, confirming or denying that she was more than concerned was useless. Shackley was convinced of it. And she wasn't trying to deny it to herself any longer, either.

"By the way, I saw to it that you still have that two bit job at Firebird's. Oh, and your lawyer called. He had an offer on your property, but thinks by holding out, he'll be able to get you more money. Said if he had had the chance to talk with you yesterday he's sure you would agree not to sell at this point. Looks like you'll be needing this job a while longer.''

Her heart did a little flip-flop at the news. She'd made it perfectly clear to Cam that the property was to be sold, as soon as possible. But that wasn't what caused the quiet rage now whirling inside her. Did Shackley think she'd sell Mackenzie down the river for a few more dollars? "I told you. I quit.''

"Well, consider yourself rehired,'' Shackley said impatiently, all traces of indulgence gone. "I'm expecting an important cable. When it comes in, I want you to take it to him.''

''I can't believe this. You seriously think you'll get him back?''

He set the coffee cup on the safe and knitted his fingers together. ''Honey, you and I know he's not happy out there on that island. He belongs in another world entirely. I'll get him back to it. I just have to get his attention first. That's where you come in.''

''Me? You already tried me. Look around you. Do you see him standing here in your office? He's not going for it. Besides, you can't want him back if his heart isn't in it.''

Shackley smiled, dismissing her comment with the wave of a hand. ''I told you, I want him back in place where he belongs, and I'll take him with or without a heart.''

Doone rubbed the edge of the cup against her lips to stop them from shaking. A chill was spreading over her scalp and down her back. Mackenzie had to be warned that Shackley wasn't simply determined to get him back, he was obsessed with the idea. He would probably stop at nothing. . . . ''I don't want anything to happen to him,'' she said, more to herself than to Shackley.

Shackley grasped his tie and choked it closer to his throat. He leaned against the four-drawer safe. ''Neither do I. The sooner I get him back, the more chance he has of . . . well, of completing the job. I'm down to the wire on this, Doone.''

Surviving was what he'd meant to say, not ''of completing the job.''

Nausea whirled in her stomach as she pictured Mackenzie alone, shot and bleeding to death. She forced back the powerful picture and fought to replace it with another one. Of him standing at the door to his inn, smiling, with the ball cap pushed back from his brow. That was where he belonged. Out on that island where he could complete his grieving and survive it like others had. Like she had after the deaths of her parents. If Mackenzie returned to the life he'd lead in Portugal he might never have the chance to see the grieving process through, even Shackley had intimated that. No matter how long it took, Mackenzie needed to know that time, still an enemy, would eventually become an ally. He had to have that chance, and she was the only one who could make sure he had it. Her decision was made in that instant. The Emerald Light Cafe could wait. She was going back to Eagle's Island to warn Mackenzie about the iron-willed man standing before her.

But she had to be careful. Shackley said he wanted her back in his employ. If he thought she'd double cross him, God only knew what the cunning man would do next to get to Mackenzie.

She scowled in mock displeasure. Shackley had to be convinced that the money he offered still held considerable appeal. Maybe even more appeal than Mackenzie.

"You really think he'll come alive again once he's back in Portugal?"

"He was undercover with military intelligence when I met him. Once those types have lived out on the edge a few years, nothing but danger can stir their blood. What's on that island to keep him going but the threat of a stubbed toe or a rabid chipmunk.

I'm telling you, I'm saving his life by giving him this chance.''

Several minutes of silence passed before she spoke. "Did Cam Ludlow mention just how much more he thought he could get for my property?'' She watched his shoulders relax as he shook his head. He'd begun taking the bait.

"Well, I wouldn't do this just for the money, you know. I mean, drug smuggling is about as evil as you can get. If you think he'll really be happy back there, uh . . .'' Hoping to appear contrite, she avoided connecting with his gaze and instead, stared at the general mess spilling across the desk. She stood and began straightening it. "But exactly how much would I get if I brought him back?''

"Honey, anything's negotiable.''

Stealing a fast glance in his direction, Doone didn't miss the gleam in his eye as he absent-mindedly spun the dial on the safe.

She drew an inward sigh of relief. He believed her. Maybe, just maybe she could pull this off.

"How's my impatient ace in the hole today?'' Shackley asked, as he stuck his head into the reception area of the Shackley Detective Agency.

Doone looked up from her checkbook and frowned. Moments before she'd been talking on the phone with Marta. At Doone's request her friend had visited Cam Ludlow's office to find out if he was in and simply avoiding her. Cam's secretary politely informed Marta that Cam was out of town and wasn't expected back for several more days. "Still impatient. I don't see why I've had to sit around this tomb of an office every day for the last week and a half. Can't you just phone me when your message comes? How much longer do you think this will take?''

''How does twenty minutes sound?'' He strode by her, an aluminum briefcase in one hand and several freshly dry cleaned tuxedos in the other.

''What?!'' Jumping up, she followed him into his office. ''The message you've been waiting for has come in?''

He nodded, jiggled the unlit cigar between his teeth, and smiled broadly. ''Now you see why I had you keep your overnight bag here next to your desk? Here, take these.'' He handed her the tuxedos and glanced at his watch. He opened his bottom desk drawer, pulled out the flannel shoe bags, and dropped them on his desk. ''I didn't send everything back to Mac. Thought they'd be safer here with me.'' Ignoring her quizzical look, he continued. ''A rental car's downstairs and the ferry leaves in seventeen minutes. And don't worry about that night job, I'll make the proper excuses, like last time. I don't care how you accomplish it, but I'm counting on you to have him back here within forty-eight hours.''

A curious mixture of exhilaration and dread streamed through her. She was going to see him again. She would take these props from Mackenzie's old nightmare if she had to, but the important thing she would bring Mackenzie was a warning—Shackley's maniacal intent to have him back. Maybe Mackenzie would believe her explanation. Maybe then she'd be able to forgive herself for opening a wound that had never properly healed. And maybe when that was done, she'd begin to understand the real strength behind her determination to help. But she couldn't think of that right now. She had a boat to catch.

Hunter clicked off the circular saw, placed it on the floor and removed his protective goggles. He slipped the goggles into his carpenter's apron and slid the stud from the sawhorses, leaning it next to several others. His guilt about Christina's death hadn't diminished, but he'd been thinking of her less often. Replacing Christina were images of Doone Daniels. He kept remembering her in vivid colors. Doone swathed in that red dress and shivering. Doone cocooned in his forest green robe and scowling. Doone cloaked in the soft blue jacket and laughing. Doone wreathed in chestnut curls and swearing like a sailor. She'd slipped into every dream for the last ten nights and those dreams had lingered throughout each new day.

He shook his head as he recalled the last moments spent with her. Why in God's name had he directed his anger toward her? She'd had the right to make that phone call to Harry Shackley no matter what the reason. And why had he come onto her so strongly in the first place? With all that she had to face in her own life, she didn't need to deal with that. If he ever saw her again, he swore he'd do it all differently. He would listen more and talk less.

"May I come in?" she asked quietly.

Hunter whirled around, his heart thudding in his chest. Was he dreaming dreams during the daylight hours now? Or was she really standing before him, her cheeks as pink as the rose colored sweater she wore? Her eyes as blue as the pleated jeans that were softly encasing her hips and legs. He blinked. Why would his subconscious conjure her up with an aluminum briefcase and an armload of packages along with several dry cleaning bags draped over her shoulder?

Doone waited, anxiety mounting with each silent second. Was he going to throw her out without so much as a word? She'd missed him so much. She blinked and the plastic-wrapped clothing began shifting down over her shoulder. "Help?"

"Doone?" He was still not willing to trust his eyes or the pounding in his chest. He rushed to the entrance way, squatted down in front of her and caught the black tuxedos just in time. While he was scrambling to keep them off the floor, she had made the same move and was now kneeling face to face with him.

Doone looked across at his stunned expression and knew in that moment that she'd done the right thing by coming back. He wouldn't send her away. She wouldn't let him. *She was falling in love with him*. If only she could take him in her arms and tell him— but by the look of confusion on his face, now wasn't the time. She dropped her armload to the floor as her hand shot to her mouth. So this was what falling in love felt like. And this explained why the standstill on the sale of her property hadn't sent her into fits. And why not having the money for the restaurant site hadn't destroyed her. Something much more important had come into her life—Hunter Mackenzie. And with him came love. She had to touch him or she'd explode from the crazy joy skyrocketing inside her. Impulsively she reached out and grabbed his hands. They were calloused and warm, and shaking the tiniest bit.

"Mackenzie, whatever it is you're thinking, you've got it all wrong."

"I do?" He looked down at her hands on his. She was holding on for dear life.

His gaze shifted to her face, his soft gray eyes tormenting her with unasked questions. "Yes, you're thinking I'm out here still working for Shackley." She took one hand away and started to ease one of the backpack straps from her shoulder.

"I am?" He reached to steady her, and felt a smile tugging at the corners of his mouth. Whether she was or wasn't working for Shackley didn't matter at the moment. She'd reentered his life with the intensity of an earthquake. All he cared about was that she'd come back, and he had never been so happy to see anyone in his life.

She sighed impatiently and fixed her gaze on the sawdust clinging to the caramel colored hair along his arms. If she wasn't getting through to him, if he didn't end up understanding everything, how would he ever learn to trust her?

"Shackley did promise to pay me, but that has nothing to do with why I'm here," she insisted, continuing to stare at his arms as she stood up. "I *didn't* come because of the money." She allowed the backpack to slide from her grip as she watched his dimples appear, then disappear. The realization that she loved him swept over her again like a warm wave of hope. She wasn't giving up on him.

"I've come to warn you, Mackenzie. You have

no idea how iron-willed Shackley is about getting you back.''

''I don't?'' The deadpan expression must be working, he thought. Her eyes were brighter, her cheeks, pinker. And the curious sensation in his chest continued to grow. He stood up and dropped the tuxedos over a sawhorse.

''No. He's got tunnel vision when it comes to you. His whole existence seems wrapped around this operation or project, or whatever you call it. The man's nuts,'' she continued, her hands splayed out in front of her. Mackenzie chewed the inside of his lip and said nothing. She stooped to pick up one of the flannel bags, then loosened the string and pulled out a shoe. ''He sits around shining your shoes,'' she said, shaking it. ''I'm supposed to be out here right now *persuading* you to go back.'' She wagged her finger. ''But I'm not. I just made him think I am.'' She waited for some sign of disbelief, all ready to reassure him she was telling the truth.

He nodded. ''I see.'' He leaned down to a Coleman cooler and opened the lid. She heard the rustle of ice cubes as he pulled out two cans of soda. ''Thirsty?''

''What? Oh. Thanks.'' She took it and continued to stare at him. He looked as if he'd accepted the information and was filing it away next to yesterday's weather. ''Did you hear what I said?''

''Every syllable,'' Hunter said, closing the lid on the cooler and twisting the catch. Shackley was the last person he wanted to talk about. He wanted to know about her. About how she had filled her days and nights since he'd last seen her. "Your ribs okay now?"

"They're fine." What was going through his mind, dismissing her almost frantic explanation with a can of soda and asking after her health like this? Did he think Harry Shackley was incapable of such determination? Didn't he care? Of course he cared. What a stupid question.

Hunter popped the top of his soda can and, as he took a hearty swallow, looked over the rim at her. "How's that perfect plan for your restaurant coming along? Did your lawyer sell the property yet?" *Is there a special man in your life? Could I make you forget him?*

She narrowed her eyes and frowned. "I'm hanging in there by a few threads. Word hasn't gotten out yet that the loft is being vacated. But, on the other hand, Cam hasn't sold the property and . . ." she trailed off as she looked up. "Aren't you going to say something about Shackley?"

"What's there to say?" he asked, meeting her gaze. "Nothing's changed." Shrugging, he chugged the soda.

Doone walked over to the cooler and placed her soda on its lid. Since the moment Shackley had told her about Mackenzie's "partner" being killed, everything had changed for her. The nameless woman's existence had provided insight into Mackenzie's actions and reactions. Finding out that Shackley wasn't going to let him alone had caused Doone to ponder how deeply she cared about Mackenzie. And now that she'd seen him, she knew just how deeply. She loved him, damn it! "What do you mean, nothing's changed?'' she asked slightly aghast. ''I've changed, Shackley's—well, Shackley's about to go over the deep end with this and—''

''Have you?''

His changing timbre seemed to alter the space between them and in one heartbeat he'd taken control of the conversation. Doone fixed her gaze on the white buttons of his faded red polo shirt. ''Yes, I've changed. This time I'm not here to persuade you to go back. That's why—''

''Why?'' he cut in softly. ''Why are you here?'' His gray eyes shimmered with quiet intensity as he waited for her response.

She turned and walked over to the tacked up blueprints of the inn and pretended to study them for a moment. *Because I love you with all my heart.* ''To let you know he doesn't intend to give up on you no matter what you want.'' She turned around to face him. ''Mackenzie, you can't imagine the look in his eyes when he talks about you. I *had* to warn you.''

''But why?''

''Because,'' she began, immersing herself in the warmth of his gentle gray gaze, ''I felt guilty about barging into your life when you didn't want anyone in it in the first place. Trying to make you come back when you weren't sure you wanted to wasn't right, either. I should have realized it sooner instead of being so selfish about my own needs.'' She felt the instant sting of color in her face and turned quickly towards the blueprints. ''I mean, my needs about the restaurant. But I was so greedy for that money that I forgot about your, uh, interests.'' She sighed loudly and turned back to face him. ''I'm here to say I'm sorry and I'm willing to stay to stall Shackley till it's too late for him to use you. It's up to you. You have a clear forty-eight hours to decide exactly what you want to do. I'll do whatever I can to help you. After that, I don't know what he'll do."

Hunter wasn't surprised by her revelations concerning his tight-lipped former boss. After more than a decade of dealing with him, Hunter could see that Shackley was running true to form. But Doone Daniels was a different matter. "With all you have going on in Seattle right now, you're willing to stay? Even after the way I treated you?" She nodded. "But I must have scared you half to death when I yanked that phone from your hand," he said, his gaze tracing the chestnut hair that appeared to dance at her shoulders with each slight movement.

She gave him a brilliant grin as the tension began dissolving. "You'd never hurt me. But you had me going there for a second."

Hunter's heart skipped a beat as he watched her stoop down and pick up a handful of sawdust. "What about after that?" She let it slip through her fingers and float to the floor like golden snow. Brushing the residue from her hands she looked up and studied him openly and thoughtfully.

"We're not so different, you and I. We hate using people. And we hate being used."

"Thank you for coming back."

She nodded before she turned to the blueprints. "You're welcome."

Hunter studied the chestnut hair rippling to her back and shoulders. It reminded him of a collection of thick ribbons, each curled on the blade of a scissor. Those shiny, decorative kinds of ribbons tied around gift packages and offered up to eager hands on birthdays and Christmas. His gaze slid down her body. Her hips shifted slightly as she leaned to press a finger against the blueprints. He cleared his throat, trying unsuccessfully to ignore the tightening sensations within him. "You seem pretty taken with those plans. Any comments?"

"Why are you putting the fireplace there?"

He crushed the soda can and tossed it into an empty Spackle container before he answered. "It's going to be the room's focal point opposite the entrance." He indicated the points on the blueprints as he stole glances at her from the corners of his eyes.

"But if you do that, few of your diners will see the sunset over the water." Sliding her fingertip over the blueprints, she continued, "If you put in a large window there instead and maybe two sets of French doors down here, you'll also have access to the patio. Then the patio doors would mirror the entrance doors. Except I see French doors aren't planned for the lobby entrance, so I guess it doesn't matter."

He pulled the blue baseball cap from his back pocket and fitted it on his head backwards, then looked at her with feigned indulgence. "What patio, young lady?"

"The one you're going to need for the tables and chairs for summer lunches. And for the deck chairs in the spring and autumn. Perfect setup for Irish coffee and hot buttered rum."

Hunter's head jutted closer to the blueprints as he studied the possibility of her off-the-cuff suggestion.

"Hmmm. And just what would you do with the fireplace?" he asked teasingly.

"Funny you should ask that," she said, playing along with his mood. "Place it in the back wall. In fact," she continued a bit more seriously as she pushed back her sleeves and raised her hands to make an imaginary frame, "you could make it a see-through fireplace, and have a cozy little barroom back there. What are your plans for that space, anyway?"

Hunter was becoming more and more intrigued with her ideas. He pulled off the cap and scratched his head. "Obviously, not what you've imagined." He pulled a tape measure from his carpenter's apron and moved across the room. After pacing off an area, he gestured for her to join him. "Hold this a second, I want to check something." After he'd taken a few measurements, he let go of the tape and she began reeling it in.

His finger slid across his lower lip for a second and then, smiling, he looked up and nodded his head. "If I'm going to have a house guest, I've got to get to town and buy some food. How'd you like to discuss this further, say, over dinner?"

"You're serious? You like my ideas that much?"

"Very much."

"Well, fine with me. But only if you let me make it," she said, walking across the room to where the aluminum briefcase sat.

He gave an exaggerated sigh of relief and held his chest. "I was afraid you wouldn't offer."

She reached down and picked up one plastic covered tuxedo. "I'll give it my best shot if you promise to dress for the occasion," she said, lifting the hanger and its contents.

She watched as he pursed his lips, looking first at the black tuxedo and then at her. Maybe she'd gone too far with the joke. He probably hadn't worn a tuxedo since his days in Portugal. Maybe she'd broken the spell they'd cast upon each other. She began to lower the tuxedo, but then she saw the twinkle in his eyes.

"Lucky for you, young lady, the mud has flaked off your red gown or you'd have to eat in the kitchen all by yourself tonight."

"I'm due for some luck," Doone said, feeling a tingling warmth spread through her body.

Hunter slipped his hands into his pockets. "I'm the lucky one," he said, then gave her a look he hoped would convey the sincerity of his words. How many men ever got a second chance with a woman like this? he wondered. "Listen, why don't you make a list of what you need, and what I don't have up at the house, I'll drive into the village and get. In the meantime, you never finished your tour of this place last week. The whole thing is finally coming together. I had a decorating firm come out and start on one of the rooms. I'd be interested in your comments. It's the first one at the top of the stairs."

Fifteen minutes later he drove away with a twenty item shopping list and a promise to be back as soon as he could. Doone scurried up the stairs of the Cliff Road Inn and looked down the long, uncarpeted hall. Each door held a brass name plate engraved with its name: Rhododendron Room, Azalea Suite, Fern Loft, etc.

Inside and to the left of a door marked Rhododendron Room she found a white pine table and two
chairs. Straight ahead was a shiny new brass bed.
The window seat was piled high with plastic and
paper bags stuffed with new bed linens, coordinated
throw pillows, and bathroom supplies.

When she was downstairs in the dining room she
had had to be content with her mind's eye, but here
were the materials to complete a decor already
decided upon. The clever design theme was keyed to
the various colors used in a set of three lithographs
hanging over the bed. The signed pictures depicted
a rhododendron in various stages of blossom. Her
fingers itched to open the bags and finish the job. It
took her all of five seconds to decide. She pushed
up the sleeves of her sweater once again and tore
into the packages.

In a matter of minutes the room had come alive
with vibrant shades of pink, warm creams, and rich
greens. She stood back to admire the cozy, yet fresh
appearance when she heard the distinct crunch of
wheels on gravel below.

Was Mackenzie back already? Rushing to the window seat, she peered through the six-paned window
to the circular drive below.

A yellow MGB with JUST MARRIED painted across
its back window pulled to a stop near the front
entrance of the inn. A man in a Navy uniform got
out, walked quickly around the small car, and opened
the passenger door. Intrigued, Doone continued watching as the smiling man helped a young woman out
of the sports car. She was wearing a white suit and
carrying a small bouquet of flowers with streaming

pastel ribbons attached. Before closing the door he took her in his arms and kissed her. It was a beautiful kiss, tender yet ardent.

Mackenzie hadn't said anything about expecting guests. Perhaps these were friends of his. In less than a minute Doone was down the stairs and out on the front deck. "Congratulations?"

The young woman nodded and adjusted the front of her suit as a blush of embarrassment colored her face.

The officer nervously twirled his hat in his hands as he spoke. "Yes, ma'am. We'd like a room for the night. The, uh, bridal suite if it's available."

"The bridal suite? Did Mr. Mackenzie promise you the bridal suite?" Had Hunter even mentioned a bridal suite?

"No. I guess I should have made reservations. But I . . . we didn't have much time. I'm Lieutenant Carson and this is my wife, Mrs. Carson. Mrs. Robert Earl Carson."

The bride added, "We decided just last night to get married. And we did—at six o'clock this morning." She looked up at her husband and smiled as she slipped her hand into his.

"We're from Oak Harbor, over on Whidbey Island. I'm going out to sea . . ." the groom's words drifted off as he returned his gaze to his bride. He studied the slim blonde then squeezed her hand. For a moment it looked as if they'd forgotten Doone was standing there. "Anyway, we heard about the Cliff Road Inn being near completion about a month ago when we were island hopping one Sunday on the ferry. We figured it had to be open by now and just took a chance that we could get the bridal suite. But it doesn't matter, we just want to be alone. Right, honey?'' Lieutenant Carson asked as he watched his bride nod.

''There is a room for us, isn't there?'' the blonde asked hopefully, not taking her eyes from her husband.

Doone scratched her temple. So Mackenzie knew nothing about this. They'd simply shown up hoping for the best. Doone looked from one to the other. The Carsons' obvious delight in each other was contagious. She watched the eager smiles the newlyweds kept exchanging. *Did her own eyes shine like this when she looked at Mackenzie?* she wondered. Was loving someone such an obvious thing? The Carsons were trusting fate to give them a few precious hours before they had to separate—and it was up to her to make a decision. What would Mackenzie do in this situation? At that moment Lieutenant Carson turned to his bride and mouthed the words ''I love you.'' Doone felt a responsive chord resonate in her chest and smiled, slipping her hands into the pockets of her pleated jeans. She'd ask Mackenzie how he would have handled it later, over dinner, after he'd come back, and after she checked the Carsons into the Rhododendron Room.

SIX

Later that afternoon Mackenzie pulled up along side the yellow sports car. Doone had been listening for him and was out of the inn and down the steps before he'd switched off the ignition.

Hunter bolted from the truck and headed for her. "Are you all right? Whose car is this?" His fingers closed over her shoulders. If anything had happened to her, he'd never forgive himself for leaving her alone.

Doone took a deep breath. No backing down now, she told herself. The Carsons were in the Rhododendron Room for the night. *And had been since their arrival!* "I'm above my average today," she finally answered, scrunching her shoulders to feel the warmth of his hands brushing her ears. "And this jazzy little number belongs to Lieutenant Carson and his wife."

"Who?" he asked, searching his memory. "Do I know them?"

"No, but I promise you this, you'll never forget them. Lieutenant and Mrs. Robert Earl Carson are your very first customers." She had felt his grip begin to relax as his fingers slid from her shoulders. Suddenly, they tightened again.

"My what?!" he asked in disbelief.

With a sheepish grin frozen to her face, she began. "Well, I couldn't turn them away. You see, his squadron's heading out to sea day after tomorrow. They were married this morning. Seems you've gotten some free advertisement by word of mouth on the weekend ferry runs and—"

"How could you do this? I'm not ready for customers."

If he'd been only angry, she would have understood, but there was an anxious tone in his voice that she hadn't expected. Where was that trust she'd begun to sense in him? Had her well-intentioned impulsiveness blown it all away? "Look, I know it sounds strange, but wait until you see them and you'll know why I couldn't turn them away. *We* couldn't turn them away," she corrected, glancing back at the second story window. "Maybe I should have said 'you.' "

"But the rooms, there's not one—"

She sighed with relief. "Oh, is that all you're worried about? Right after you left I found the Rhododendron Room and it was practically begging for minimal chambermaid attention. I couldn't resist. It's a perfect bridal suite."

He shot her an exasperated look.

"Doone, the sheet rock's not even up in the dining room."

She folded her arms across her middle, fighting the growing tension in the air. "They want to eat in their room. Don't be so upset. Look on the bright side, your open sign has yet to be painted and already you have paying guests.'' The fact that the bill would be paid with a personal check by a person leaving the country seemed immaterial at the moment.

Hunter stared up at the second floor windows. ''The nets. The nets aren't up on the tennis courts yet.'' He could ring her pretty little neck for this. He wasn't ready to take this step, and it had nothing to do with unfinished tennis courts or properly painted signs either. He just wasn't ready.

''Shhhh! They'll hear you. Mackenzie, they're on their honeymoon, and it only lasts until tomorrow. Tennis is the last sport they have on their minds. You'll understand why I had to let them stay when you meet them.'' The image of the newlyweds' kiss, and the groom's silently spoken ''I love you'' flashed through her mind. At that moment, Mackenzie twisted around to look at her with a comical air of total exasperation, and she felt the corners of her mouth lift in response. After all, who didn't understand love when they saw it right in front of them? In the meantime, she had dinner for four to prepare. ''You know what I think? I think as an innkeeper, your first night jitters far outweigh theirs. Relax, Mackenzie, and trust me.'' She looked into the truck, then back at him. ''Did you get everything on the list?''

''What? Yes.'' He planted his hands on his hips. ''You know, you're crazy? Do you ever stop and think things through?''

''Not really crazy. Impulsive.'' Leaning across the seat she began dragging a sack of groceries into her arms. "And practical, of course. I sure hope you have a jar of paprika."

His gaze settled on her backside. "Why?" he asked, momentarily distracted from his anger.

She looked back over her shoulder, shaking her head. "Because, Mr. Twenty Questions, you have guests who are upstairs right now working up an appetite. Bring down a jar from the house when you bring my dress, okay? I figured, as long as the inn's stove is hooked up, I'll cook here. I already brought down the pots and dishes from the house. By the way, I'd get this place soundproofed as soon as possible."

She handed him the grocery sack and reached into the truck for a second. Hunter adjusted the bag onto one hip, pointed a finger at her and inhaled sharply. Soundproofed? At this point he was afraid to ask. But he'd get to the bottom of that later. He was learning there was no stopping her once she was on a roll.

Hunter watched Doone wipe a dab of flour from her nose. Since he'd gone to change into his tuxedo she'd pulled up her hair and secured it with a huge barrette. Suddenly, as if she'd sensed his presence, she turned around and gasped, allowing several of those little ribbons of hair to escape. He'd been leaning against the stainless steel refrigerator door enjoying her deft movements for the last few minutes. Totally absorbed in boning and skinning the chicken breasts, she hadn't heard him come in through the back entrance.

"Do you always whistle while you're wielding a

knife?'' He hung her red silk dress on a cabinet knob and awkwardly placed four wine glasses on the butcher block.

"Always. How long have you been standing there, uh, listening?'' She watched him unbutton his tuxedo jacket, pull a corkscrew from his cummerbund and reach for a bottle of wine.

"For a while.'' He uncorked the bottle. "A good chablis, just like you ordered.'' He closed his eyes and sniffed the cork. "A very good chablis.''

"You look so . . . nice.'' Doone turned back to the work area. Had confetti been swirling around him she wouldn't have been the least bit surprised. He was absolutely the most gorgeous man she'd ever seen, and her hands were shaking so hard she had to press them firmly against the countertop to still them. He looked like something out of an Aramis advertisement with his hand-tied black bow tie around the neck of his pearl-studded white silk shirt. The tuxedo fit his wide shoulders and long muscular physique as if it had been tailor-made for him, which it probably had been. She glanced down at her clothing and winced. Flour liberally decorating her from nose to knee, she was sure even Julia Child would have rejected her. Sighing, she brushed the front of her jeans. His glamorous "partner'' certainly had never looked like this. She stared at the platter of floured chicken breasts. Could he ever love an unemployed chef with a penchant for impulsiveness as much as she loved him?

"Hey,'' he said softly, "are you okay?'' He'd come up behind her, and even though his voice was low, she jumped and turned to face him.

"Fine. I was just thinking about . . . paprika."
The two glasses of wine he was holding caught and
reflected the crisp pleats in his shirt along with her
floured sweater. She winced again. "Paprika's got to
have a bite to it . . . did you know that?" He smiled
and shook his head. "Well, I'm not surprised," she
mumbled absently, totally lost in his smile. "Most
people can buy a can . . . keep it on the shelf for
years without . . . ever knowing that fact."

He nodded. "Guilty."

She blinked. "What?"

He lifted the glasses away from his body. "Reach
in the inside breast pocket. Go ahead," he urged,
"tell me the bad news about my paprika."

She wiped her hands on a paper towel, then gingerly lifted the lapel of his jacket, and felt for the
pocket. "There doesn't seem to be anything in
here." She stepped closer for a better look. "Maybe
it's—"

"Come here," he whispered, stopping her words
with a kiss. And then another. He *smelled* better than
Aramis. Doone slipped her hands inside his jacket
and forgot about everything but the taste and feel of
him. She'd been waiting for this forever. "Closer,"
she heard him whisper, as he succeeded in overwhelming all of her senses. She pressed closer and
felt his body quicken right before they heard the
thumping crash overhead.

He immediately broke the kiss and pulled back.
"What the hell was that?" Wine splashed from the
glasses he was still holding and he quickly set them
down.

Grabbing a bag from the counter, she held it up

near his chin. "Do you think you could slice these onions for me?"

He pushed aside the bag as he made his way quickly toward the service doors. "Not until I find out what that noise was."

"Mackenzie, wait!" She fixed her eyes on the small paper bag wishing she could crawl inside it. Having to listen to the newlyweds exercising their libidos overhead had been bad enough while she was alone, but now that Mackenzie was here, and hearing it as well, was totally unnerving! "It's the Carsons. I, uh . . . They've been a little, uh, frisky for the last hour or so." He pursed his lips as if to stave off a smile.

"Frisky?" Recognition suddenly shown in his eyes. "Ah, yes, the soundproofing."

Maybe she could dump out the onions and pull the bag over her head. Pretending to ignore his question, she reached for a knife and set it down beside the bag of onions. "I think while you're slicing these I'll slip into the pantry and change my dress." She grabbed the dress and made a beeline for the door.

"Tell me something." He watched her hesitate, then turn around to face him. Scarlet still glowed in her cheeks.

"Yes?"

"Do I have to whistle while I do it?"

"You're going to make me die of embarrassment, aren't you, you rat!"

He laughed softly, then winced as another thump sounded overhead. "How did you get us into this?" He pulled an onion from the bag, tossed it in the air, and caught it. "What made you do it, Doone?"

She heard the thoughtfulness in his tone and asked cautiously, "Do what?"

"What really made you rent out the room?"

She backed slowly toward the pantry door. "Love."

"Love?" He pronounced it like a foreign word from an ancient language as he set the onion on the counter. "What about love?"

"How old are you?" she asked, feigning exasperation.

"Thirty-eight, uh, thirty-nine, I mean." He'd had a birthday in the last month or so, but like so many things, hadn't bothered to take note of it.

"Thirty-nine? Well, you must have been in love at least once during those thirty-nine years." She backed through the swinging door and disappeared.

"Just promise me you'll never act on your romantic notions again," he said loudly as he chopped into the onion.

"We were speaking of love, not romantic notions. And you haven't answered my question." She stuck her head out the door and lowered her voice. "You've been in love, haven't you?"

He pulled a small jar of paprika from his back pocket and set it next to a container of sour cream. "Mind if I try fending off these personal questions until after we've had our dinner?"

"Do I have a choice?"

He began to whistle as he picked up the knife and made a clean slice through the second onion.

They'd taken their own dinners back to his house and had eaten there. Afterwards, Doone kicked off her heels and settled herself on the rug in front of the fireplace. From her joyful memories of her parents, to the embarrassing and costly affair with Bailey Swift, she'd filled him in on her life's history. Throughout their dinner, he'd insisted he wanted to know everything and prompted her through the telling with nods and smiles, and a gentle squeeze of her hand now and then. She'd shared the many facets of her life before tonight with her friend and landlady, Marta, and a few other close friends, but somehow she knew they'd never understood in quite the way Mackenzie seemed to. She pulled up a knee and rested her chin on it. Now it was time to hear about him. There had to be a way of easing him into a beginning without sacrificing the intimacy between them. And the growing trust. She looked back over her shoulder at him sitting in the rocker.

"You handled it perfectly, Innkeeper Mackenzie," she finally said, referring to the comical scene after they'd waited a full five minutes, dinner trays in hand, for the Carsons to open the door. "Have you always been so suave with breathless guests? Mixing business with pleasure, I mean." She turned back to the fire and winced. That didn't come out exactly like she'd wanted.

Hunter watched the quivering flares of firelight showing through the ribbons of her hair. He'd been imagining how it would feel to remove the barrette, allowing the rest of her hair to escape before he captured the wanton mass in his hands. If she only knew what she was doing to him, all female and shimmering like this. He leaned back in the rocker, finished his wine in one long swallow and set down the glass.

"Have I always been so suave with my breathless guests? Is that what you asked? I can remember a rainy night not too long ago when someone breathless showed up on my doorstep. I wouldn't call my behavior then all that suave, would you?" The sound of her soft laughter warmed him and he tipped his head back and smiled for a moment. "You were right about the Carsons. There was no way I could have turned them away," he said, then added thoughtfully, "The lieutenant has a lot of lonely months ahead of him on that aircraft carrier."

Doone leaned forward and wrapped her arms around her bent knee. "She's going to be just as lonely, Mackenzie. Especially after such a little while of . . . being together." She shook her head. "It isn't fair."

Sometimes nothing was fair, Hunter thought. It wasn't fair, he mused half seriously, that he had had to share her with the newlyweds today when he'd just gotten her back. But every once in a while, something incredible happened that seemed to make up for all the unfairness. Something as incredible as the way she made him feel tonight. She'd shared the story of her life and somehow made him feel a part of it. When she'd described the joy at each of her father's homecomings or the giddy pranks she'd played upon a strict ballet teacher with her boarding school friends, he'd laughed along with her. And when she'd described the horror of learning about her parents' death, his heart had suddenly become heavy. Then there was that Swift character. He'd seen the hint of confusion in her eyes when she'd spoken of him. God only knew what Swift had done to her. As Hunter studied her now, she reached up and opened the barrette. Thick chestnut hair dropped down to cover her shoulders. He wanted her at this moment more than he'd ever wanted anything or anyone.

Doone watched from the corner of her eye as he left the rocker, removed his jacket, and sat down beside her. The silence seemed to resonate with a rich and growing tension. Together they turned to look at each other. The haunting sadness in his eyes was gone, replaced by trust.

His look was a silken cord that wrapped around her, drawing her closer and closer. Tilting her head, he kissed her so sweetly that her eyes filled with tears. One slipped over his finger.

"Doone Daniels, I won't make love to you if you're going to cry."

She rose up on her knees. "Then kiss my tears away, kiss them all away."

And he did. With sweet, torturous control. "Doone," he whispered with each perfect kiss. His eyes were bright and soft and magically vital as he lifted his head and looked into her eyes once again. At that moment she would have given him her heart, but it was already gone. He'd stolen it with that melting look and was dragging it back on that silken cord.

Doone reached to take him in her arms. Then hesitated. The fires in his smoke gray eyes were demanding everything. Could the desire to please him be enough to insure it? Once before that hadn't been the case. A sinking feeling began to overtake the joy that had been blossoming within her. She studied his long, strong fingers splayed across his thighs. To have come so close and not know him the way she hungered to was like dying before the first breath was ever taken. But to gamble and fail in the act would be worse.

In searching for the courage to tell him, she closed her eyes. But shutting out his image didn't help. She *wanted* to look at him, drink him in, know him. She looked into eyes—and the words tumbled out abruptly, "I don't know how to be a lover."

"You've never—"

"I might as well have never. I'm afraid I won't . . . be enough of a woman for you." She turned away and thought about Bailey Swift and his stinging appraisals. "I'd rather die than tell you this."

Hunter's smile verged on tender laughter. "But you're never afraid of anything." Yet he saw that the small agony still veiled her face. What had that selfish clod in her past done to make her doubt this precious right of womanhood?

Doone watched as he drew back and got to his feet. So he didn't want her after all. He didn't want someone who didn't know how to make love. She felt as if a cold blanket of needles were wrapping around her, pressing in each painful memory, holding her back from the man she loved. He'd given up on her.

He watched as her hands went to cover her face and he took them, pulling her to her feet. Lifting her chin on the side of his finger, he studied the hundred things her eyes were asking him. A smile worked itself up from his chest and settled at the corners of his mouth. "I won't rush. And I won't hurt you."

He took one of her hands, peeled back her fingers, and lowered his mouth to her palm.

The sensation of his lips pressed there spread through her body like forked lightning. His breath was as soft and warm as cashmere laid across her skin when he whispered, "Let me be the one to show you you're woman enough."

Spellbound by his ardent plea, she wordlessly received the press of his lips against her throat, then her chin and finally, adoringly, her mouth. The pleasure was instant and strong as it sunk steadily into her body and plundered its way to her core.

"Tell me you trust me, Doone."

He ran his lips back and forth against hers, stifling her protest. "I only need to hear that you trust me. Tell me that you do."

Nothing mattered but to be in his arms. Nothing. There was no past and no future. Only this night, only this moment, only this man. "I do."

She watched as he loosened his tie then turned off the lights and removed the cummerbund. He reached for the pearl studs in his tuxedo shirt next, then looked up and smiled.

"Will you help me with these?"

Doone nodded, grateful for a chance to busy her nervous hands. Her fingers touched and lingered with his as they removed the shirt and finally tossed it aside. Everything seemed to slip into slow motion when she returned her gaze to him. In the sepia firelight, his body glowed warm and tempting. The light hair covering his broad chest was surprisingly soft when she reached up to touch it. She ran her fingers down his chest thinking, *this is all so right.*

He covered her hand with his and held it hard against his chest. Then he kissed her. "Turn around and lift up your hair." She obeyed him wordlessly.

Unhooking her dress, he lowered it, ready to remove her bra. His mouth went dry and for a moment he couldn't speak. She wasn't wearing one. He fleetingly noticed the firelight deepening the tan of his hands—hands that contrasted with the warm ivory flesh of her breasts as he turned her back around and lowered the dress further. He held the red silk at her hips as he filled his eyes with her. She was more than his dreams had promised. He swallowed. "Do you know . . . do you have any idea . . . just how beautiful you are?"

"Hunter—" His name felt like warm honey rising in her throat. He slid the dress and her panties from her hips, then steadied her as she stepped out of them. She straightened while his gaze slowly strayed over her nakedness, touching, stroking, caressing her relentlessly. Then he met her eyes, his expression suddenly sad with surprise. "You really don't know, do you?"

She believed him. She believed that he thought she was beautiful. Desire swirled through her like a frantic mass of butterflies; their softly beating wings tempting her body with a need that only he could provide for her, filling her soul with a mystery that only he could solve.

In all the important ways, he knew, this would be her first time. And that pleased him more than he could say. He lifted her hair and pushed it behind her ears, surprising himself as his hand displayed the tiniest tremor. That had never happened to him before.

He bent his head to the rosy-hued circle of her nipple, capturing it with his mouth, demanding its attention with his tongue. Impudently resisting at first, the moistened pink pearl began responding—as he had wanted it to.

Doone held her breath, but his languid pace continued. Moving her fingers into the golden hair at his temples, her shoulders moved, restlessly weaving an invitation for him to continue. A strong and deepening pleasure streamed through her, and she wondered vaguely at her body's powerful response to such gentleness. When his mouth strayed to the other rosy allurement, repeating the sweet torment, she swayed against him, wondering no more. She knew this was how it was supposed to be.

He felt her move once, twice against his thigh, and desire, already gripping him, burgeoned higher. The need to wrap himself in her intimate embrace and share the bittersweet sensations thundered through him like a raging storm. He fought the impulse to hurry—*he couldn't do that to her*. Then he was kissing her arms and breasts, his fingers lightly tracing her waist and hips. He cupped the lush curves of her bottom, drawing her against the hard evidence of his need. ''No one could want you more than I do. And no one's going to know you the way I will.'' Slipping his fingertips into the moistness between her thighs, his voice became a promising murmur. ''Every beautiful inch of you.'' Slowly, steadily he worked his fingers deeper into the honeyed satin and felt her melt a little more.

Pleasure coursed through her in a flood tide of sensations as she gasped with the accuracy of each feathery, tantalizing stroke. His tongue rimmed the delicate shell of her ear, replicating the erotic gesture of his fingers and this time she shivered. Gently flexing her knees, she allowed his slow hand more to explore, more to know, more to pleasure. With a teasing hesitancy he held back, barely touching the dewy folds. She dragged both her hands down his arm to squeeze at the flexing cords of his wrist. Why was he holding back? She licked her lips and looked up. Why didn't he do something . . . anything to stop this madness . . . or to continue it? "Hunter," she moaned indelicately. But his fingers continued their slow, magical perusal, teasing her with promises to be fulfilled. "Hunter."

His words were hot and demanding as he whispered them against her ear: "Say it." His hands slipped up the silky indentation of her spine as he repeated the words over her eyelids, down her cheeks, and over her lips.

Say what? What was she suppose to say?! Her hands curled into fists, and she stroked them against the swell of his biceps as if to push him away. *But she wanted him closer*. And she wanted him closer . . . *now*. "Please. Now."

The sound of her voice, thick and sweet, twisted through him, heightening his desire to a fever pitch. At this point he didn't know who was shaking more, and he didn't care. He removed the rest of his clothes and quickly drew her down. "We don't have to hurry," he lied. How had he ever thought he could control the passions she stirred in him?

She brushed the red dress out of the way and pulled him back against the rug. "Yes, we do."

He could have taken her swiftly then, but that trusting look remained in her eyes, reminding him of his promise. He entered her slowly, shuddering as he sheathed himself in the sweet, darkness of her heat. He looked into her eyes and when he could, he spoke. "Do you trust me?" She nodded. "Then hold me close."

Doone pressed her hands to the small of his back and closed her eyes. The room suddenly felt as if it were spinning, and when she opened her eyes he was on his back and she was astride him. She grabbed his shoulders and pushed up to protest the position. And froze. Without warning the pleasure swelled within her and her mouth opened in sensual response to it.

"Trust yourself," he whispered fervently.

Looking down at the smoldering desire in his eyes, she knew she could deny him nothing. She began to move, slowly at first. With each breathy sigh, with each small circle she drew with her hips she invited him higher and higher. His face was hunger and love and joy, and instinctively she began to know it was a reflection of her own. Her eyelids began drifting shut as the spiralling pleasure tightened convulsively within her.

Hunter watched her eyes close. He had to know all of her when the moment came. He had to know the depths of her passion and the heights of her pleasure. "Open your eyes." She opened them and he saw her look of astonishment as the first shudder of ecstasy tumbled through her. She cried out his name and he was there for her. Fleetingly he realized that he was the first to witness the perfection of her ecstasy, the first to hear her cry out from it, and he gloried in the knowledge.

He'd wanted her pleasure to go on and on, but as the primal rhythm she played with her hips increased, the last of his tenuous control began to flee. He tried calling it back with her name, but the word dissolved into a dark oath. And then he was over the edge and into the oblivion of bliss . . . with her. Wave after surging wave of pleasureful release erupted from him. He spent himself inside her, surrendering a part of his soul and all of his heart.

With one last shudder Doone dropped her head onto the high hollow of his shoulder. He held her, stroking her hair and whispering endearments. For a long time she lay close and quiet in his arms savoring the mellifluous sensations.

"Hunter?"

He eased her alongside him, then ran his fingertips over the light sheen of moisture between her breasts before he kissed her there. The small gesture stirred him with a shocking quickness. "Yes?"

"I . . . you know, I'll listen if there's anything you want to say. You haven't talked about . . . you know you can trust me to listen."

Hunter's gaze left her breast and returned to her face. In that moment he realized he could easily have worshiped her. It would have been so easy to—he knew it by the aching pleasure that came from deep inside his heart. He could have worshiped her brilliant blue eyes if they just didn't hold that unwavering trust. He could have worshiped her lips, except

for the tear quivering there. He could have worshiped
her body if she wasn't so near, trembling,
waiting. . . . But worship demanded a distance—a
distance he could no longer endure. Once he could
have worshiped her, but now, God help him, he
could only love her.

"I know—" he began, but the rest of his sentence
was lost against her lips. He would tell her all of it,
but not now. Now he needed to touch her again, to
hear her cry out again, to love her again.

He didn't have to persuade her this time. Doone's
need matched his with an urgent response that surprised them both. He didn't have to say he loved
her, either. The message was in his touch and in his
look. It was in the way he waited; it was in the way
he couldn't wait. And afterwards, when he kissed
her with an almost reverent gentleness, she knew the
words weren't necessary. But somewhere a part of
her listened for them anyway.

His body eclipsed the pale firelight as he stood and
scooped her up into his arms. She didn't care where
he took her as long as he was with her, as long as
he didn't leave her. Running her fingertips along the
steel hard muscles of his shoulders, she smiled, wondering what a third time would be like.

Entering the hallway on the way to the bathroom,
he shifted her weight. They'd shower, he told himself, then slip into bed and sleep. Tomorrow morning
he would answer those questions that needed answering. This intimacy couldn't go any further until she
knew. . . . She nipped him softly on the shoulder,
then licked the sting, and nipped him again. Her
fingertips sank into his hair as she pulled his head

toward hers and kissed him. Hunter closed his eyes and swallowed, but desire for her was already rivering through him once again. "Doone?"

"Mmm?"

"Doone!?"

Her fingers roved the area between his collar bone and nipple. "Yes, darling?"

"Do you know what you're doing to me?"

"I hope so," she said a little breathlessly before taking half his ear into the moist interior of her mouth.

"You'd better stop that," he said with little conviction.

"Make me." The certainness in her voice transcended the challenge of her words.

"Doone . . ." he began as he allowed her to slip from his arms onto her feet. He drew her into the bathroom and turned on the shower. When he'd pulled her inside the large steamy enclosure he looked down into her face. "I want you again," he said almost apologetically.

She licked the water droplets from her lips. "How? Show me how."

SEVEN

Sensing his presence in the first rousing moments of consciousness, Doone jerked her head from the pillow toward the figure beside the bed. Coming out of the nightmare, the panicky feeling continued as the fully clothed masculine form suddenly loomed over her and began to speak.

"Good morning, sleepyhead."

"Mackenzie!" she cried out, then reached up and grabbed the brown leather sleeve, pulling him toward her.

Relief flooded into her voice. "Mackenzie, you're all right."

"Of course I am." He stroked her brow with the back of his fingers. "Sweetheart, what is it? What's wrong?"

"I . . . it was nothing. A dream." Her hand slid down the worn jacket sleeve and closed over his hand. "Come here." He levered himself over her length, taking most of his weight on his knees and arms. The sound of crushed leather and the smell of his aftershave distanced her further from the nightmare. She kissed him quickly. Here, in all of her senses was Mackenzie. Hadn't her heart always felt like this, hadn't she always loved him? There was nothing to fear now. The stupid dream was only that, a dream. "You're dressed and you've already shaved. Where were you?"

He planted bent elbows on either side of her and wriggled his fingers. "Do these dishpan hands tell you anything?"

"Oh no. The dishes and the pots and pans." A weak smile of exaggerated apology crossed her face, as she propped herself up on her elbows. "You did them."

"I did. I also checked the Carsons out of the honeymoon suite." He fumbled in his pocket, then dropped a check onto the sheet covering her breasts. A look of amusement crossed his face. "My first check as an innkeeper. Which I've been asked not to cash until next Tuesday."

She ruffled his hair and squealed softly. "Oh! That's wonderful. You must be so happy."

"Very happy." Entwining his fingers in her hair, he leaned in to kiss her, but stopped at the last moment. Dampness still clung to her hair reminding him of her startled awakening. "Oh, Doone."

"What?" She kissed him lazily.

"The dream you had must have been a nasty one. Why don't you tell me about it?"

Lightness had gone out of his voice, replaced with a concern that touched her. "It was crazy," she began, running her fingertips along the zipper teeth of his jacket. "One of those surreal things. You were someplace away from me, but you weren't really. I had to get to you, but I couldn't find you. Then you were behind something; I think it was a tree trunk or a building. But it wasn't.'' She looked up. ''See, it's not worth remem—''

Hunter pushed up and away from her. He sat on the edge of the bed, feeling himself sinking into a vortex of symbols. Symbols, he realized, that could easily signify his past . . . or maybe his future. With an almost macabre sense of curiosity he said, ''Go on.''

She studied his profile, and the far away look in his eye. He really meant for her to continue. ''There was an animal in it, a huge animal with beautiful fur, and it was clawing at you, tearing pieces from you. I kept hitting it with my fists, but it was oblivious to me.'' She remembered the terror she'd experienced as she dreamed and the words began tumbling out. ''I've never felt so helpless in my life. I couldn't get to you. I kept shouting that you had a knife. It flashed in your hand, but you didn't see it, didn't even know you had it. Then the two of you fell away. You were . . . gone.'' She forced a breathless laugh. ''See? Wasn't that stupid?''

Slowly standing up, he took off his jacket and tossed it aside. He shoved his fingers through the top of his hair. ''I think your dream was your subconscious trying to give you some answers about me. Answers I should have given you last week.'' He turned to look at her. ''Harry Shackley didn't choose you just because you were desperate for money. He chose you because you resemble my partner. Her hair was straighter than yours, straight as a new paint brush and darker. As dark as your hair looks when it's wet. And she had brown eyes."

Doone felt a sickening sensation in her chest. Her heart was hammering in her throat. "You were supposed to think of her when you saw me. When you—?"

Hunter snorted softly and shook his head. "Harry's a manipulative bastard, but you and I know that what happened last night belongs to us. It will always belong to us." A crooked little smile appeared on her face and Hunter felt something crumble inside him. Always didn't seem long enough.

"I won't interrupt again. Please, go on."

"I had gotten word to Shackley that the job called for more help than I had, and he sent her to me. She was too young and inexperienced for the operation, and I told him that. But he said headquarters insisted that she was an asset and that she stay in place. He said that no one would be suspicious of a beautiful young woman who came to live with me. And no one was."

Doone's skin prickled along the back of her spine. *She had lived in his house.* The thought burned inside her as other images followed. *She had slept in his bed. She had given him love and she had taken his.* Doone cleared her throat. But that was all over. It had to be. "What was her name?"

"Christina."

Christina. The name seemed to echo of gold and crystal. Doone closed her eyes. Royal. Steadfast. And his, she thought.

"I told her to stay at the house that night, but she didn't listen. She never listened. She just walked into it. Gunfire and knives." He shook his head. "I should have sent her back the day she came, no matter what Harry or headquarters wanted. And I'll have to live with that until the day I die." He stared off again, remembering the rest of it.

Doone watched him, her heart splintering in tiny pieces with each silent second. He had to get it out, all of it, or he'd never get past it. "Is that when you got the scar?" she asked as evenly as she could.

He nodded, taking an enormous breath as he did. "I tried to get to her, but I didn't make it in time. She died because of me. It's as if I pulled the trigger, as if I murdered her. She'd be alive today if I—"

"No!"

"Yes. It's true, Doone. I could have done something to prevent her death. If I'd held that meeting in a different grotto down the coast, or made certain she hadn't followed me that night she'd be alive. She was my responsibility."

Doone scrambled off the bed and went to him. "Don't you say that." He turned his face away, but she pulled it back. "You listen to me. It was an accident. A lousy accident. If you insist on taking the blame, then you at least have to share it with some other people, Mackenzie. Shackley, for insisting you keep her. The government, for not training her well enough. And maybe she should have been more careful."

"It wasn't her fault, it was mine."

"Mackenzie, I understand how you must have felt about her. Unless there's something you're not telling me, there's no good reason to continue punishing yourself. Even if you can't see it wasn't your fault, you've got to forgive yourself; you've got to do that and get on with your life."

Hunter stared into her relentless blue gaze, and saw an earnestness that made his heart leap. "What did I do to deserve you?" They were in each others arms in an instant, his face buried in her hair, her hands stroking him.

"You can't slip back into that life." She drew away and looked up at the faint smile forming on his lips. "I couldn't bear to lose you."

The look in his eyes was unreadable, but the emotion behind it was both deep and compelling. Doone remembered the look. He'd had it the first night she'd met him as he'd looked up from reading the documents.

"Everything's going to be fine, Doone."

"Not until you've told Shackley to go to hell," she said smoothly, as she picked up his robe from a nearby chair and slipped it on. She turned and headed toward the bed. "And I want to be there to see it." After fluffing both pillows and tossing them into place, she reached to straighten the comforter. "We have time to catch the morning ferry, if we hurry."

He'd followed her across the room. "It's Saturday," Doone heard him say as she felt his arms go around her waist. She leaned back into his solid embrace and drew in a deep breath. Everything *was* going to be fine.

"There's an afternoon ferry. We don't have to hurry," he whispered, pushing the robe from one of her shoulders and slowly kissing her there.

"Hunter," Doone sighed, reaching back to stroke the outside of his thighs. He pressed her against him, leaving her no doubt as to his intentions. She turned in his arms and the robe cascaded to the floor. "How come I'm the one who's naked first again?" she teased as they both unbuttoned his shirt.

He shrugged out of it and with a roguish grin on his face, reached for his belt buckle. "Because you're prettier to look at."

Hunter drove Doone's rental car at breakneck speed toward the ferry terminal in Evergreen Village. She wrapped her arms around the Irish setter sprawled across her lap as Hunter pulled the car in front of a small frame house about one hundred yards from the dock. Turning off the ignition, he nodded toward the man on the ladder leaning against the house.

"Come on and meet my father."

"That's your father? But, he was the one who went over the directions to your place with me the first night. He never said—" Sheeba began pawing to be let out, and Doone reached for the door handle.

"Wait, Doone. I'd, uh, rather you not say anything about your connection with Shackley. The mere mention of Shackley sends him for his heart medicine."

Doone looked at Hunter and then at the man outside. "How will you explain why I've been here twice in two weeks."

"I don't think that's going to be necessary." He leaned closer, whispering, "One look at you and he'll know. Now get out of this car before I start to kiss you again."

Doone opened the door, waited a split second for Sheeba to exit, then got out herself.

"For God's sake, Dad. You know the doctor would be furious if he knew what you were up to." Hunter moved forward to steady the ladder as his father started to climb down.

A good-natured smile lit the old man's face. "So it's you, is it? I was up fixing a few of my shingles."

"Well, you should have waited until I got down here to fix them. I did stop by yesterday, by the way, but you were out. Dad, this is Doone Daniels, but I understand you two already met."

"You didn't tell me you were his father, Mr. Mackenzie," Doone said, reaching to take the senior Mackenzie's hand.

He winked. "Call me Al. Guess I forgot to mention that fact."

"You also forgot that I didn't want anyone up there, Dad."

"Plug in your phone."

Al Mackenzie's expression suddenly softened and a mischievous grin crossed his face. "Must have been a full house at your place last night with that other young couple, too."

Al Mackenzie, Doone noted, gestured with his chin in much the same way as his son. "Those two are over there smooching in their car waiting to board the ferry."

"Dad, I'm going to Seattle for a few days," interjected Hunter before his father could continue. "Would you mind?" he asked, as they all looked down at the prancing dog. Sheeba woofed.

"Of course not. Sheeba's always welcome here," he said, playfully cuffing the animal. In the distance the ferry signalled its arrival with a sudden blast of its whistle.

"Thanks, I'll go get her food."

"No need to. I'm sure I've got dog food from last time."

"Well, I brought some extra. It wouldn't hurt to have it here." Mackenzie opened the back door of the automobile and pulled out a sack of dog food. "Let me get it in the kitchen for you, Dad."

"Son, that's enough food for a month of . . ." He stopped in mid-sentence and turned to Doone. The warmth in his eyes vanished and all of the light-heartedness of the past few minutes vanished with it. He shook his head in disgust.

"Harry Shackley sent you, didn't he?"

She hadn't anticipated this, or the guilty feeling cascading over her like an icy shower. Before she could reply, Hunter walked between them.

"Dad? I need to see you alone. Now."

Hunter followed him into the house, dropped the sack to the floor, and closed the door. "This is the last time, Dad. I'm settling it for good with Shackley. I mean it. You'll never hear of him or from him again."

"And I'm suppose to believe that with you up at your place dragging your heels for a year . . . waiting for something to happen. Hunter, for God's sake, I've never stood in your way, but you've got to get those years behind you."

Hunter laid a hand on his father's sagging shoulder. "This won't take long, Dad."

Al Mackenzie looked toward the door. "Is she what's making you do this?"

Hunter shook his head. "Not in the way you think. Like I said, I'm coming back."

A few agonizing minutes later, Doone watched the two men emerge from the house. Al Mackenzie looked at his son for a long moment and then slowly nodded to Doone. She had hoped for more than a wordless acceptance. But considering the years Hunter had spent apart from his father in connection with Harry Shackley, it was understandable that Al Mackenzie would remain suspicious of her.

Hunter pulled a leash from his jacket, attached it to Sheeba's collar, and handed it to his father. "Let's go, Doone."

An uneasiness quivered through her as they got back into the car, bought their tickets, and drove onto the ferry. Something wasn't quite right. She followed Mackenzie from the car deck, up the central staircase, and across the observation deck of the ferry. "What did you two talk about in th—"

"Wave to him, Doone." Together they waved to his father.

Sheeba let out a heartrending howl. "Keep her off your bed, Dad," he shouted.

Doone looked across at Hunter's profile and smiled. Last night and this morning rushed back in details warm and bright. Everything was fine, she reminded herself, as his arm went around her. It would only be a matter of time before he would leave it behind him for good.

The hum of the boat's engine increased to an almost menacing vibration. Water churned and foamed around the hull and the gap between the ferry and Mackenzie's father widened. Impulsively, Doone leaned over the railing, shouting, "We'll be back soon." The older man smiled at last and waved.

Once they met with Shackley their lives would ease back into place as effortlessly as the ferry gliding over the deep waters of Puget Sound. The Emerald Light Cafe and the Cliff Road Inn seemed near enough to touch and smell. Sure and steady as she'd ever been about anything, Doone laid her head against Mackenzie's shoulder and ached with happiness.

In a series of stops and starts they wound their way through the open stalls of Seattle's Public Market. From the flower stalls at the north end, through the artfully arrayed vegetable section and finally to the fresh seafood displays, the circuslike atmosphere swept them along. Alaskan King crabs stacked like interlocking bricks on a bed of crushed ice brought Doone to a standstill. She rubbed her hands together as she spotted a mound of bisque colored clams and glistening black mussels on an adjoining table. "I sense a great *paella* in your future, Mackenzie."

No sooner had she spoken than a vendor wearing an oversized apron came around to the front of the pile. He pulled two crabs from the stack. "Fresh off the boat this morning," he said loudly.

Hunter wrapped one arm around Doone's waist and whisked her from the spot. "Cook's day off."

"Forty eight hours, I can guarantee forty eight hours of fresh crab." The vendor raised the two crabs shoulder high, then higher still. His voice carried far into the crowded aisle.

"But I *am* hungry," she protested laughingly.

Hunter pulled her past a pair of street musicians playing bawdy folk songs and around a somersaulting clown before he drew her into a narrow passageway. Pressing her up against the wall, he held her there with the full length of his body.

"Hungry for what exactly?" he whispered, nuzzling his mouth against her throat.

"You," she laughed. "You, you, you!"

"Hey, Mac," someone called out.

Doone felt his body freeze into an almost protective shield around her. Their shiny bubble of joy had suddenly vanished. She peered over his shoulder and let out her breath as two men shook hands a few feet away. "It was someone else, he wasn't calling you. Is everything all right?"

He eased away, checking behind him as he did. "Serves me right trying to ravish you in a public place." His smile returned as he lifted her hand to his lips and kissed it. "Didn't you say you had to call your landlady?" She nodded. "There's a phone in here," he explained, guiding her down the passageway toward a restaurant at the end.

Five minutes later Hunter watched from a table near the top of the stairs as Doone hung up the phone and made her way up. She stopped at the dessert cart to study the petite fours, eclairs, and multiple layer cakes before continuing to their table. One moment she was as determined a businesswoman as he'd ever encountered, and the next, she was like a kid at a carnival, he thought. But the best thing of all was that she was his. For now. And, maybe . . .

"Marta says Cam Ludlow called last night. He wants me to meet him tonight to talk over the sale of my property. Cross your fingers for me, this could be it." With a satisfied sigh she sat down and looked over his shoulder at the seagulls outside the open window. They flew in gentle swoops and shallow dives in the warm spring afternoon.

Smiling, she moved the vase of yellow daffodils and the cup of cappuccino aside and touched the light, crisp hair on the back of his hand. "I don't think I ever told you the name I've picked out for my restaurant. It's the Emerald Light Cafe. You know, because Seattle's official nickname is the Emerald City. What are you looking at?"

"You." He wanted every hair, every pore, every eyelash burned into his memory. When the time came for him to . . . Doone suddenly shivered.

"What is it?"

"Only the wind picking up off the bay."

Hunter took a deep breath. He'd never believed such intuitive relationships existed. But it was happening with them. Either that or she had figured out his next step. Or . . . he was wrong and she'd simply taken a chill from the open window.

Hunter forced a deadpan look onto his face. "Probably getting excited about seeing your loyal attorney this evening."

Doone lifted the cup to her mouth and blew gently on the cinnamon dusted froth. She stared at one deepening dimple alongside of Hunter's mouth as she thought of Cam and his tortoise shell glasses. She shook her head in amusement. "Cameron Ludlow is about as exciting as a dish of vanilla pudding. And speaking of food, what did you order for lunch?"

"Here it is now," he said, moving aside his cup

and saucer. The waiter placed their lunches before them. "Hot seafood salad and the house wine. I assumed, by your slavering reaction to those king crabs, that seafood would be a safe bet."

"You were right. You're always right." Beneath the damask table cloth, she slipped her foot from her shoe and ran it up the inside of his calf. "But I'd be a pretty boring person if my appetites were always that predictable," she teased. She watched as he popped a cherry tomato into his mouth and smiled back at her. "You do agree, that being consistent is much more important than being predictable, don't you?" Her foot slipped higher.

Hunter reached between his legs and grabbed her by the toes. "I don't know what the hell you're talking about, but I promise to survive this lunch for your very thorough explanation."

"My pleasure," she said primly, easing her foot to the floor. Of course he wasn't going away, going back to that life. Because if he went away, he might not . . . What a ridiculous thought. It was such a stupid, ungrounded fear anyway, now that he'd explained everything. And they *were* going to see Shackley. Out of sight of Hunter's gaze, she flicked the hemmed edge of her napkin with a set of nervous fingers. Most new love must be like this—little unexpected moments when paranoia seemed to slip in and wreak havoc with the newly found balance in your heart.

She looked across the table as Hunter winked, popped another cherry tomato into his mouth, and then forked in a shrimp. God, what was she worried about?! Any man who ate like this couldn't be planning to go undercover to catch drug smugglers. Or to immerse himself in the memories of a dead lover, either!

"I've got to get myself a razor. It's been such a long time since I've needed one that I forgot to pack one this morning."

Normal talk. Everyday talk. The tension began dissolving from the center of her chest. "No problem. I have one at my place."

"Please." He pressed his hands together in a prayer like manner. "The last time I borrowed a lady's razor, she'd shaved her legs with it and . . ." In the next instant his smile disappeared. His gaze fell on the flower arrangement at the next table, and he blew softly through his lips. Faux pas didn't get any worse than this.

Doone propped her elbow on the edge of the table and lowered her forehead against her palm. Their situation certainly was unique. How much longer before the memory of Christina would leave him in peace. And her, too.

Mackenzie shifted in his chair and cleared his throat. "I usually get a room at the Mayflower Park when I'm in town. I think just for tonight I'm going to do that."

"You don't have to. You don't have to do anything you don't want to."

But I do, he thought to himself. Hunter dragged his finger along his bottom lip before he spoke. "Look, wouldn't it be easier if I wasn't there when your lawyer shows up?"

He had a point. This long awaited meeting with Cam Ludlow had to be strictly business. If she had to explain Hunter Mackenzie to him, her attorney would be so busy concerning himself with Mackenzie's character and background, she was certain he'd never get to the sale of her property. After all, Cam Ludlow was the one who'd "saved" her at the last minute from marrying Bailey Swift. Doone closed her eyes, remembering the well-researched dossier Cam had pressed into her hands the night before the wedding. She nodded to Hunter. "A lot easier."

"Besides, if my father needs anything, he knows he can reach me at that hotel. You can pick me up there in the morning and we can go to Shackley's office then." That's what she wanted to hear, the part about going to Shackley's. He forced a smile and leaned back in his chair, assured that he appeared totally relaxed. Totally honest. Like the old days, he told himself. How easily it all came back. Deceiving. Manipulating. Lying. He looked away from her.

She knew he made perfect sense, of course. So why did she feel so uneasy about being separated from him? She could suggest that she join him at the hotel tonight after her meeting with Cam. But *he* could have suggested that. And he hadn't. She looked away from him.

"Let's have dessert. After that, how about another look at those crabs or clowns or whatever it was that made you laugh before. And then I want to see the location you've picked out for the Emerald Light Cafe," Hunter said, hoping he'd recaptured the magic.

EIGHT

Doone replaced her Lauren perfume in the wicker basket on her makeup table, and looked once again at the business card she'd propped against the mirror. How many men owned a fountain pen anymore, and used it? she wondered, grinning and shaking her head. Since returning from the Public Market and finding Cameron Ludlow's card on her doorstep, she'd reread it at least a half dozen times. *DD—A special night for a special person. My favorite restaurant at seven thirty—yours, CTL,III.*

The elegantly scripted message teased at her mercilessly. Cam had finally seen to the selling of her property, that had to be the "special" part. He might even have a nice fat check with him tonight. Peering into the mirror, she pulled at the padded shoulders of her black velvet dinner dress, smoothed back an errant lock and attempted to rub off some of the color on her cheeks. It wasn't coming off, and neither were the freckles. She laughed at her reflection; sunburns had a habit of staying for awhile.

She thought back to the sunny hours she'd just spent with Mackenzie at the Public Market. They'd taken their time, savoring the sights and sounds and smells as they meandered through the crowds after their lunch. She closed her eyes, remembering and cherishing moments with giddy delight.

He bought her a single earring shaped like the Space Needle.

She put it on, happily dangling it for him whenever he kissed her.

He fed her chocolate-dipped strawberries from his fingers.

She tossed popcorn to the seagulls, then to the pigeons, and finally at him.

He scooped her up, threatening to drop her into the bay.

She scurried away, her shrieks lost in the happy din of the afternoon.

He followed her along the market's upper level past babies in backpacks, camera-toting tourists, and an organ grinder with a tiny monkey. They made their way down the angled stairs, past the warrenlike shops and straight to the future site of the Emerald Light Cafe.

And when she showed him its perfect size and breathtaking view, he ignored the present greasy-spoon atmosphere and pronounced her choice brilliant. He sat down on a rickety chair, pulled her onto his lap, and listened to her plan.

"Can't you just picture it, Mackenzie?"

"Every detail. Even those Finnish vases with the crackled glass."

Finally, he said it was getting late and he had Cliff

Road Inn business he ought to see about. Hand in hand, they'd made their way up the oddly-junctioned stairs and back to the rental car. He'd taken out his overnight bag and kissed her, saying he would see her soon. She'd leaned against the car and watched him head up Pine Street.

Reaching across the makeup table for her pearl earrings, she caught a glimpse of the souvenir earring in the mirror. The inexpensive bauble tickled her neck reminding her of Mackenzie's surprise kisses that afternoon. Damn it, she didn't care that the earring didn't "go" with the short, black velvet dress. She wanted a reminder of Mackenzie with her, and this would do the trick. Snatching up her purse, she did something she hadn't done in years. She stuck out her tongue at her reflection, putting the last of those nagging little worries in their proper place. After all, everything appeared to be working out at last. Tonight, Cam Ludlow would probably present her with that big fat check she'd been counting on. Even Harry Shackley owed her money. The Emerald Light Cafe would soon be hers, and Mackenzie . . . oh, Mackenzie. There were no words to describe her love for him. She clicked off the little lamp on her makeup table and said a prayer of thanks. Life had never been so sweet, so rich, so full of promise.

Twenty minutes later Doone entered the palm-banked entrance of one of Seattle's finest hotels. The fawn suede walls and gleaming crystal lamps gave the illusion of shadowed velvet and opulent wealth. Approaching the entranceway to the dining rooms, Doone rolled her eyes as she listened to the clicking of her heels against marble. Cam Ludlow could pick the strangest places to conduct, what had become over the years, casual conversations about her legal affairs. He was like an older brother, and more often than not, an overly protective one. Standing around on that Elliott Bay cruise ship last autumn while being introduced to Seattle's leading politicians was not the place she'd envisioned herself while telling him about her idea of opening a restaurant. He'd actually spilled champagne on himself when she'd told him.

"Madame, have you a reservation?" asked the maitre d' as he lifted his gold pen to an open book.

Doone peered past an enormous arrangement of calla lilies and into the main salon. "I'm meeting a Mr. Ludlow at seven-thirty."

The maitre d's ramrod posture bowed backward and his chin lifted a fraction higher as he heard the name. "Of course, Mr. Ludlow left word to show . . . Miss Daniels, isn't it? Yes. To show you to his table. Right this way please."

Well, if he insisted. But she wouldn't have any trouble spotting Cam in this sort of setting. It didn't matter that half the men in the room were wearing tuxedos, Cam Ludlow had probably worn one to his own christening. In fact, she'd never seen Cam without his shirt neatly and totally buttoned and his tie knotted with the precision of a military officer standing inspection. He was a stickler for details, just the person she needed to take care of selling the property.

Cameron Thurston Ludlow, III, rose from the mauve colored chair and buttoned his jacket. "Doone, dear, you look absolutely ravishing. I'd never dreamed black would become you so.'' He waited with a benign smile as the maitre d' seated Doone. Then he unbuttoned his jacket and retook his chair.

"Thank you. Hello, Cam,'' she began pleasantly.

"Hello? That's all? Not hello, I've missed you?''

How about hello, why haven't you returned my calls? she wanted to say, but he was here now and with good news, she was sure. "Cam, about that cryptic note I found on my doorstep tonight. Can I assume the real estate firm in Boston has good news about—''

"Now, now," he said with a placating gruffness, "let's have a drink first. Waiter? Two scotch rocks here.'' He turned back to Doone. "I have a surprise for you.''

This was it, the check from the buyers, the check that would finance the Emerald Light Cafe. She watched as he lifted the mounded napkin beside his plate and pulled out a miniature nosegay of silk violets. Placing them on the gold-edged china plate between her elbows, he continued. "Of course, these seem a bit delicate with that dramatic dress. Not that the dress isn't attractive, but I would like to think of you in something more, shall we say, demure?''

Shall we say beige, Cam? Doone thought. What business was it of his how she dressed? She narrowed her gaze at him as he smoothed an imaginary wrinkle from the front of his shirt, then straightened his bow tie. Mackenzie wore formal attire as if it were his second skin, but Cam looked stiff in his. He always looked stiff, as a matter of fact. She continued to stare at Cameron Ludlow as she thought about Mackenzie alone in a hotel room a few blocks away.

"With a look like that, you certainly know how to unnerve a fellow." He folded his arms and crossed his legs. "But, tell me, little one, how have you been keeping busy? Tsk, tsk. That isn't a sunburn I see, is it?"

Doone let out an undisguised sigh. "I work, Cam, I don't sit around keeping busy. I *am* busy." Cam had known her for years, but Mackenzie, knowing her for only two weeks wouldn't have to ask if she was keeping busy. And as for the sunburn, it went rather nicely with Mackenzie's callouses, thank you very much. She glared at Cam, amazed at how irritating he had become.

"That's it. That's what's got you so overwrought tonight. You just haven't had enough leisure time. I should have made arrangements to see that you were taken care of while I was away. One of my partners keeps an apartment in Friday Harbor—"

Doone drummed her fingernails on the tablecloth. The man listened as well as a certain Irish setter she knew. "Cameron, I happen to be an adult. Where did you get the ridiculous misconception that I need a baby sitter or a social director?"

Cameron ran his finger around the inside of his collar. "Doone, I've always seen to what's best for you."

She rubbed her forehead. So far this meeting had been a waste of time—time she could be spending with Mackenzie. "Right now, we need to discuss the sale of my property."

He nodded, affecting a suspiciously serious expression. "I only want to see you happy."

She spoke through gritted teeth. "Then tell me

you've had my house and property sold so I can go ahead and lease the site for my restaurant.''

"Oh, yes, the restaurant again,'' he began in a gratingly condescending manner. He paused as the waiter delivered their drinks. "Doone, I've thought this through thoroughly and I have a much better plan for you. A plan that includes a secure and successful future. In fact, a virtually problem-free life. It's time I see to it that you're settled down.''

"I don't know what you are talking about. The restaurant *is* my future and—'' She stopped short, deciding it prudent not to mention Mackenzie. The conversation had become complicated enough without including him. "Every time I try to bring up the restaurant, you simply hold your breath waiting for the idea to pass or rush into some idea of your own.'' She took a deep breath and stared him straight in the eye. "Now, have you sold my house and property or haven't you?''

"I found it in your best interest not to put the property up for sale.''

For one horrible moment she couldn't breathe. Impossible. But, by the cocky tilt of his chin, she knew Cam Ludlow was telling the truth. She started to her feet. *"What?! All this time . . . wasted?!"*

"Doone, dear, don't you think you should lower your voice?'' he asked, shadowing his brow with the palm of his hand.

"No!''

"I didn't want to say it like this,'' he said, getting out of his chair and coming half way around to her side of the table, "but my feelings for you have deepened over the years. This restaurant idea of yours was unsuitable from the start, yet until you became insistent about it, until you gave up a perfectly responsible career in advertising, I had no idea how much I—I've grown to love you." He reached for her hand, and in a momentary daze, she allowed him to take it. "A politician's wife would have no business running a restaurant. You know you've always had a certain class about you that even this self-imposed poverty never tarnished—"

"Wife?! Love?!" she fumed, jerking back her hand. Heedless of the stares coming from every table in the room, she continued. "I trusted you like a brother. How could you? Manipulating my life like this? Oooooh! I should have known from those political parties you dragged me to exactly what you were up to. Well, I'm not a wandering waif in need of a guardian any more, let alone interested in a marriage of convenience for you."

"Now just a minute," he began, affecting a charade of bruised pride. "You gave me reason to believe there was something growing between us."

Aghast, she stared back. "What? No, I didn't. And until your political star suddenly started to rise—that's it, isn't it?—you were quite content to play the good family lawyer. I trusted you. And don't tell me again that you love me, Mr. Promising Politician. That would be quite unethical on your part." She leaned in, placing both hands on the table. "And while I'm handing out the free advice, next time you zero in on a woman, make sure she likes scotch. I never did. And, as for these," she continued, snatching up the silk violets, "I hate artificial anything!" Before his saucer like eyes, she tossed the nosegay dartlike into the glass. "And I wouldn't vote for you if you were running against Godzilla." Grabbing her evening purse, she turned on her heel to leave.

"Doone, for God's sake, will you wait a moment?"

She looked over her squared shoulder and caught a glimpse of him holding onto a dripping mess of dark purple silk.

"Wait? Never again Cameron Ludlow. I'm done waiting."

"Madame, please," begged the maitre d', patting his forehead with a linen napkin he'd snatched from a nearby table. "Is there something, anything I can do to calm this situation? Please, madame?"

"Yes, there is. You may call a taxi for me. Mr. Ludlow's party of two has been cancelled. Permanently."

The maitre d' hurried after her, passing tables filled with silent diners staring in undisguised awe. "And where, madame, will this taxi be taking you?" he asked in a rush of relief as they reached the palm court.

Doone looked out of the revolving brass and glass door. A true Seattle spring night had settled in as a thin, silvery rain softened the automobile lights in the street outside. She smiled warmly. "To the Mayflower Park Hotel."

"It's open," Hunter called out.

Doone twisted the knob and pushed open the door. She looked across the shadow-filled hotel room. Hunter was resting his forehead on the rain beaded wall of glass. One of his sock-clad feet was crossed over the other and balanced on the curl of its toes. She studied the tableau of his solitary figure silhouetted against the reflections of red and yellow lights. Her heart seemed to catch in her throat. He took a sip from his glass. He was far, far away.

Watching him like this was like listening to a never-ending sigh. Her hands clenched involuntarily. She had been right to come. But her appearance wasn't going to be the flighty moment of surprise for him as she'd imagined it would be. It was obvious his mind had drifted to sad thoughts, probably of the past. Well, he didn't have to endure them alone, or much longer for that matter. After their meeting with Harry Shackley tomorrow, it would all be different. She smiled softly. Wonderfully different.

Doone watched him a moment longer. He reached over his shoulder to rub the scarred area through his shirt. Private thoughts were one thing, private hell was another. He was hurting tonight. Mentally and physically. No, damn it, he wasn't going to spend the night with old ghosts. Old ghosts couldn't massage your back. Old ghosts couldn't listen. Old ghosts couldn't love you. But she could.

He still hadn't bothered to turn himself around. "You can put it by the door," he murmured, sipping the drink again.

"You don't sound very hungry to me, Mr. Mackenzie," she said, wheeling in the room service cart and closing the door.

"My God," he breathed, pulling away from the window, away from the streaming, blood-like beads of rain. After focusing on her reflection, he whirled around.

"We must start working on your welcome. All those potential customers that are about to clamor up the steps of the Cliff Road Inn are going to clamor right back down them again, if you insist on greeting them like this." She turned to close the door.

Images of Portugal and mostly Christina were filling Hunter's mind that evening. It was time to face the past and deal with it, not forget it. Not yet, anyway. So each time Doone had come into his thoughts, he had forced her out. But that was no longer possible. Not when he heard the light laughter in her voice. Not when he caught sight of the satiny flesh of her back framed in the soft, deep drape of that black velvet thing she was wearing. Not when her presence swirled with the fresh memories of this morning, of today, of yesterday, of last night, of . . . Hunter swallowed hard. He shouldn't let Doone stay and he knew it. There were things to be done, things that she couldn't be involved in. "I thought we agreed to be apart tonight."

Doone felt a prickling shock up and down her spine, the kind of feeling she'd always associated with sudden fear. No matter how the rest of their afternoon had turned out, at lunch he had said that he would see her tomorrow—not tonight. Insecurity and humiliation came crashing down around her. Her lips parted with the soft shock of embarrassment from her impulsive behavior. It was a capricious act showing up at his hotel room like this. He didn't need to hear about dinner with Cameron Ludlow and the revelations that came with it. Would she ever learn to look before she jumped? The bottom line was, he needed a buffer of solitude before tomorrow's meeting with Harry Shackley. The very bottom line was, he needed tonight for himself, and probably for Christina. Doone blew out softly through her lips.

"You're right," she began in a whisper. "I shouldn't have come here tonight. Considering what has to be done tomorrow, you probably want to be alone. I'm sorry I barged in." She turned to the door, twisted the knob, and pulled. "Room service said to leave the cart—"

He was beside her in an instant slamming his hand against the partially opened door. "Come here," he whispered fiercely. In that same moment, he pulled her into his arms and covered her mouth with his. "Stay," he murmured when he could bear to take his mouth from hers. "I need you to stay."

Wrapped in his welcoming embrace, pressed against his wide, warm chest, she burrowed her body against the length of him. He pressed his lips against her face, her throat, her mouth. Closer, her body seemed to scream. She felt his body respond with undeniable evidence of his arousal. Honey flowed to her center as he pressed his growing hardness against her. "Mackenzie?" Then she whispered his name again, softly this time. "Ahh, Mackenzie."

Hunter crushed the edges of the black velvet that draped her back as he swayed her in a silent dance of desire. "Talk to me. Let me hear you talk, let me hear you laugh." *Push back tomorrow. Make tonight last forever.*

Doone nuzzled against the underside of his chin, tasting the hair-prickled skin of his throat. Was it laughter he needed? Or was it loving? She felt an erotic energy rushing to every nerve ending in her body. "I can do that."

"You can, can you?" he commented indulgently, his fingers trickling encouragement down her back. "Then talk to me."

Doone stepped out of their embrace and kicked off her shoes. "Turn around," she ordered, ignoring his tone as she flicked her fingers in his direction.

"What?"

"Just turn around."

He turned.

She reached up underneath her dress, peeled the panty hose from her legs and feet and tossed them onto the dresser. Reaching for the dress's short length of zipper near the base of her spine, she smiled with relief when it gave on the first tug. A dress whose time had come . . . and gone, she thought, peeling the long sleeves down her arms.

"Doone, I'm not hearing anyth—" His breath caught in his throat as he heard the zipper give and then something soft fall to the floor.

He heard her giggle deliciously. "You can turn around now."

Those shadowy memories of minutes before were wiped away by the sight before him. He leaned back against the door. The sparkle in her eyes, the way she was nibbling her lips, her creamy curvy flesh punctuated by her erect nipples . . . and the triangle of dark curls at the apex of her thighs hardened him to aching. "Don't you ever blush?" he asked, his gaze raking the sleek curves that framed his temptation.

"You didn't teach me that last night. Or this morning either."

He pursed his lips as he fought back a smile. "Hmmm. Well, would you like me to see what I can do about that now?"

"No."

"No?"

"No. Actually, I've just decided to seduce you. So I guess it's up to *me* to make *you* blush."

Hunter ran his tongue along the inside of his cheek and raised his brows. "And you're going to talk while you do this?" He tucked his thumbs into his belt loops, leaned against the door again, and waited. "It's your seduction," he urged, watching the fleeting look of indecision crossing her face. "Uh, you will let me know if you need some help, won't you?"

"Possibly," she replied, her courage returning with each of his reassuring gazes—gazes that seemed to caress every inch of her. She ran her hands partway down her thighs and watched how his lips parted in an inaudible gasp. "You know what Tiger Daniels always said?"

He blinked, then met his gaze. "Fly high and fast?"

"I mean, as my father."

"Uh, never date a pilot?"

She closed the space between them with two slow steps.

" 'If you want something badly enough, go after it with everything you've got.' "

Hunter dropped his chin and stared down his nose

at her. "I knew I loved that guy. You're a lot shorter without those heels, you know."

"They say it doesn't matter when you're lying down." Doone reached up to unbutton his shirt. She moistened her lips. "Do you think it matters?" She gave his shirt a rough tug pulling it out of the waistband of his trousers.

He swallowed. "Does what matter?"

"Never mind." She unbuckled his belt and loosened the catch on his trousers. "Nice material," she remarked, running her fingertips up the inseam. "I see you went clothes shopping this evening."

"I did?" He cleared his throat. "Yes, I did."

"And you've gotten a haircut? Looks awfully good. Stylish."

Hunter raised both his hands to plow them through his freshly cut hair and was taken completely by surprise as she pushed back his shirt and circled one of his nipples with her tongue. He sucked in his stomach in instant response and called on heaven to help him.

"Amazing," she continued, in a devilishly conversational tone. "How can your skin be so, so . . ." she stopped to kiss the center of his chest, "hot, when you haven't even had a . . . sweater on. Did you buy a sweater, too?" Her hips squirmed lightly against his erection.

"A sweater? Yyesss, I bought one of those." He lowered his hands to touch her thighs.

"You know, I didn't wear a coat tonight," she said, stepping back out of his reach. "Do you think I could borrow that sweater a little later?"

"You can have it. I'll buy you a dozen," he said,

as he removed his shirt and slipped off his remaining clothing.

She leaned back against the dresser, making sure he watched as she dangled the souvenir earring with one finger. "What color sweater did you get?" she asked, as he awkwardly stripped off his socks.

He smiled. "Red. About a shade darker than the color of your nose and cheeks." God help him, he'd almost asked her to leave. Asked her to leave? He scooped her up in his arms and walked toward the bed. "Am I blushing yet?" he asked, laying her gently down on the riotous floral print spread.

"Well, parts of you are."

He leaned his hard length against her thigh and laughed. "Parts of you are, too," he said, covering one of her nipples with his fingertips.

The rain could cry against the window all night long, she thought. They were wrapped in a rainbow of joy and desire. And trust. Thrusting her fingers into his hair, she urged him closer. She met his gaze and gently shook her head. "Oh, the things I've done since meeting you, Mackenzie!"

"Go on, tell me about those things," he said, before he dragged his tongue along her collar bone. He moved his mouth down to one tightened nipple and closed, sucking gently.

She twisted closer, moving restlessly against him. "Big chances. Crazy, wonderful . . . thrill . . . ahh!"

"They're the best chances to take," he said, as his fingers moved over her belly, down through the triangle of curls to lightly feather over the inside of her thighs. She reached for his hand and took it higher. Liquid fire flooded his loins as he slipped his finger inside her. "You're so ready," he breathed, trying to control the frenzy clearly about to overtake them.

She stroked the front of his hip, daring closer to his hardness with each pass of her hand. A plea, an answer, an affirmation of their shared desire came sweetly to his ears. "Yes."

His breathing was ragged now. "Touch me." She wrapped her hand around him and for one glorious moment he forgot to breathe. Then he levered himself into the cradle of her thighs, lifted her hand away, and entered her in one gliding stroke. And knew immediately he wasn't going to last much longer. He felt spring cocked and ready to explode as he delivered his urgent message in two soft gasps. "I'm so close, don't move."

"I don't want to wait." She pulled him closer with her knees, but it was the intimate embrace of her honeyed center and her husky command that made him groan his surrender. "Don't make me wait, Hunter."

He didn't. Through it all she heard irreverent oaths, desperate prayers, and then, at the pinnacle of desire, her name. An explosion of ecstasy broke over them, cascading through their oneness like a shimmering August star shower.

Minutes later when she was finally able to breathe normally, she moved her head to kiss him. His breathing was steady and deep. She smiled to herself, brushed back a damp curl from his forehead and hugged him carefully.

"I love you, Mackenzie. I love you, I love you, I love you."

She would, she told herself, tell him again in the morning. Before they went to Shackley's. She closed her eyes.

When he was certain she was sleeping soundly, he carefully lifted himself from her embrace. In the darkness he found his trousers and pulled them on. He located the bottle of bourbon and the plastic cup on the rug by the window and poured himself a drink.

"I know," he finally whispered back, then turned away to look out on the city.

The next morning Doone sat on the edge of the bed, pulling apart the flaky layers of a croissant, while she waited for Mackenzie to finish his shower. He was taking forever. She tapped her bare toes on the rug and looked at her watch and then over at the bowl of strawberries and small pitcher of cream. Mackenzie's romantic gesture of having breakfast waiting at her bedside when she awakened had delighted her. It had been at least fifteen minutes since she'd awakened and she'd yet to see him to tell him thank you.

A little anxiously this time, Doone checked her watch. Ten thirty. She reached for the coffee pot, but instead stood up and went to the bathroom door. "Hunter, if you're in there, say something." She waited a few tense seconds before she pounded on it. The sound of the shower was all she heard. "Hunter, I'm opening this door." She opened it, went in, and pulled back the shower curtain. He wasn't there. With her heart pounding in her chest, she rushed back into the bedroom seeking some sign of his presence. But there was nothing. The closet was empty, too. Even his overnight bag was gone from the collapsible rack near the foot of the bed. He had left her.

NINE

Ten minutes later she stepped into a cab parked outside the hotel and hurriedly gave the driver directions to Shackley's office. She still couldn't manage to put her finger on it, but something about Hunter going alone to Shackley's office sent a shiver through her. They were supposed to do this together. Doone leaned forward in the taxi and tapped the driver on the shoulder. "Please, could you drive a little faster. It's very important."

"Lady, I'll drive faster, but I think you missed the ball," he said, eyeing her black velvet dress in the morning light.

Doone ignored the comment and the cold vinyl against her spine as she sank back into the seat and closed her eyes. Something was wrong. Something was terribly wrong. Last night he'd loved her as if . . . there would be no tomorrow. But there was a tomorrow. It was here, right now.

"Relax, nothing's wrong," she chanted to herself fifteen minutes later as the elevator doors opened.

Hurrying across the hall, she twisted the doorknob, shoved it open, and stepped into the reception area. He probably wanted to spare her the scene with Shackley. Her heart felt as if it were dissolving in her chest when she heard the muffled voices arguing in Shackley's office.

"None of your business how she managed it. Let me see the new cable traffic," she heard Hunter say. Quietly, she opened the door to Shackley's inner office.

"Luis never caught on that you were anything but a casino manager who wanted to make extra money dealing drugs. He never suspected you had both governments behind you. He probably thinks you're on some island off the coast of Spain still recuperating. Your cover is holding, Mac." Shackley tossed a file folder toward Hunter. "Here. Take a good look at that last cable, and then tell me what you think." Shackley leaned back in his chair and brought a lighter near the tip of his cigar. The lighter misfired as his eyes focused on Doone. "Daniels, what the hell are you doing here?"

She'd come. Hunter swore under his breath, but didn't turn around. With a stony silence, he pulled himself up from the huddled position over the desk and shoved both hands into his trouser pockets. Get out, he silently willed her. Get out, now.

Ignoring Shackley's question, Doone moved toward the desk. It was still the same messy desk. The same Styrofoam coffee cups, the same ashtray overflowing with unlit cigars and tobacco bits. But she noted this almost unconsciously. Her eyes were on the broad, straight shoulders of Hunter Mackenzie's jacket.

Now that his hair had been cut, a margin of flesh showed between his hairline and the collar of his yellow, oxford cloth shirt. A margin of flesh she couldn't recall ever kissing. Her eyes snapped shut.

"Have you told him yet?" she asked.

The bulldog jowls shook as Shackley tossed the lighter to the desk and pointed the still unlit cigar at Mackenzie. "Told me what?"

Mackenzie's head came up slowly and Doone watched the muscle in his jaw move. He reached for the file and opened it. Without looking at either of them, he began reading.

She reached out to grasp his arm. "Why are you doing this? You don't have to—"

"Harry?" he said without looking up from the papers in his hand.

"What the hell is this all about, Mac? Spill it."

"Pay her."

She stared up at Hunter and the steady gray eyes that hadn't bothered to meet hers. It wasn't true! He wasn't going back. He wasn't going to end what he'd so lovingly begun. "Hunter. Stop this. It's all behind you. Hunter, look at me!" Her voice was a frightened whisper.

He glanced toward the window, then to Shackley.

She hurried to speak, both her hands encircling his forearm. "You have a new life now, a reason not to go back." Her fingers continued clutching the soft wool of his new navy blazer. "Don't do this to yourself."

She snatched the file from his hands, threw it on the desk, and grabbed both his wrists, forcing him to look at her. Was there a wavering in those nickel gray eyes? "Hunter, please say something."

Shackley rolled the cigar between his thumb and forefinger. "Mac, you won't get this chance again. Take her with you if you want. Just don't back out now."

He turned to Harry. "We're playing hardball here. Leave her out of it." The answer was quietly lethal, totally unyielding. Then he turned to Doone. "Let go."

"Listen to me, please. I know we should have talked about it last night. I'm sorry. But we can talk about it now."

Make it good, Mackenzie, he told himself. He looked down at her fingers, they were white knuckled and trembling. "I don't want to hurt you. Let go. Now."

Shackley spoke next. His voice overly confident, he said breezily, "You see, I told you he'd come back."

Breaking her grip, Mackenzie lunged across the desk sending files, cups, and an overloaded ashtray in every direction. He yanked Harry Shackley from his chair. "Shut up," he hissed.

Doone steadied herself against the paint-chipped file cabinet. The two men continued arguing but Doone couldn't hear them for her own loud thoughts. Pointed cruelty, at least, demanded careful attention from the giver. But Mackenzie had nothing more to offer, she realized. He'd given in to the morbidity of his past, and, in doing so, had given up on the two of them.

I should be bleeding, she thought wildly. He's

turning me inside out and I should be bleeding. What was real? These two strangers before her? Had the past few days been a dream? A cold, sharp pain nicked her heart as one word pulsed through her mind. Used. Used. Used. Who was this man with whom she had so willingly shared her secrets? Who was this man that she'd cradled in her arms, invited into her body, and welcomed into her hopes, her dreams, her soul? She looked again at Hunter Mackenzie as a nameless emotion gripped her. He'd planned to leave her all along. He'd never actually promised her he wouldn't.

She waited for the wave of nausea to pass. "Was I good, Mackenzie?"

His head snapped around, his brows knotted together questioningly.

She spoke again. "Was I as good as Christina?"

Hunter let go of Shackley's lapels and stood up. He studied the agony in her icy blue eyes. The insecurity of her past was flooding in again, drowning the once incredible warmth in her eyes. He had the words to end that agony right now. The words to make it right again. But he couldn't say them. God forgive him. "No, you weren't."

Perhaps the numbness that enveloped her was something to be grateful for. The real pain would begin soon enough. Not the simple, easily understood kind that came from a stupid mistake. No, nothing involving Hunter Mackenzie was simple.

Her shock still buffered with numbness, Doone nodded and looked at Shackley. "My work appears to be finished here. If you'll pay me, I'll be gone." She walked past Mackenzie ignoring his stare.

"Right. I'll put a check in the mail this afternoon," said Shackley. "By the way, I called the restaurant where you hostess and gave them a good story. Your Aunt Babs from Albuquerque passed on to that cactus garden in the sky, and you're to be back from the funeral sometime this week. They expect you at the restaurant Thursday at six, so show up with a turquoise ring or something. In fact, if you want to make it look real good, I'd even suggest—"

"Cash. You promised me cash," she said, slapping her evening bag on the desk. "I'm not in the mood to wait, either."

Her eyes narrowed with a vengeance that made Harry Shackley blink. She watched as he glanced up at Hunter and then back again at her.

Doone squared her shoulders and looked toward Hunter. "Did you think I'd melt like sugar candy in the rain?"

Hunter swallowed quietly. She was going to make it. That gutsy look in her eyes was back and that was all the evidence he needed. She'd been through hell and back again before, and she was going to survive this, too. After what he'd just done to her, there was some consolation in that thought, thank God. "Give her the money, Harry. She earned it."

Shackley rolled his chair around to the safe behind his desk and twisted the dial. Soon he plunked down a heavy gray metal box on his desk and opened it. Stacks of neatly wrapped bills were removed and one at a time tossed across the desk to her.

Doone began to count it.

"Trust me, it's all there."

It was Harry Shackley who'd made the comment, but Doone turned her gaze from the money to Hunter Mackenzie.

"What a joke. Pretty funny, don't you think so, Mackenzie? Well, don't you think it's funny? Trust." When he didn't reply, she shoved the money into her purse and headed for the door. And didn't look back. She'd die if she did that. Or worse, she might beg him, again, to stay.

Four nights later Doone was stopped by her landlady, Marta, halfway up the stairs to her apartment. "You look not so good, my friend. Come in and tell me where you have been."

Her landlady's apartment smelled, as always, of warm apples and furniture polish. Of home. "I apologize for not helping with the children's ballet classes this week."

"I thought I heard you upstairs several times in the week. You could have told me you had your lover with you. I understand such things. But a week? No wonder you look so tired." Marta's eyes widened and an impish grin stole across her face.

"Marta, I spent this week alone."

"Alone?" Marta's arm went around Doone's shoulders. "Are you ill?"

Doone shook her head. "Just a little depressed. I got fired. Actually, I'm out of two jobs now. Are you getting all this? Am I going too fast?"

"Yes. But it is a good thing for my English." Marta motioned Doone to the huge, claw footed dining room table. "Sit down. I have coffee.

"Important cups for important conversation, yes?"

Marta said, placing a coffee tray on the table a few moments later.

Doone nodded, lifting one of the creamy white cups with the hand painted roses. She needed to talk, and who better than Marta? "Very important, Marta. But these are so beautiful and fragile. Are you sure you want—"

"My favorite tenant, tonight you are, as ever, beautiful, but something about you is fragile, yes? I think perhaps this is not the cafe of your dreams of which you are truly disturbed. Nor these jobs that are no more. It is this man you spoke to me of the other week?"

Doone nodded. She'd told Marta about Mackenzie after she'd returned from the island the first time. Telling Marta about him was like telling a favorite aunt. All understanding, no judgement and plenty of pep talk.

"Ahh. The man you gave your heart to."

"And I can't seem to get it back," Doone whispered as fresh tears streamed down her face. "I never thought I could let anyone hurt me like he has. Marta, I can't believe I'm still such a poor judge of character when it comes to men. Even my lawyer."

"That lawyer, Mr. Ludlow? What has he done?"

"It's what he hasn't done, he never put that real estate up for sale. He even tried to convince me he didn't do it because he's in love with me."

"But, this sounds like a Hollywood movie," Marta commented, as she reached for a box of Kleenex.

"Wait," Doone added sardonically. "It gets better." Then she told Marta about Hunter Mackenzie and the fake detective she no longer worked for.

"Experience *is* the best teacher and I've learned my lesson well. Hunter Mackenzie took two weeks out of my life, and he's not going to take any more! I'll never trust those adolescent . . . feelings again. I'm going to be stronger for surviving this, Marta," she said, taking the box of Kleenex into her arms. With a self-deprecating laugh, she added, "After I finish these tissues, anyway." She sniffed, and leaned back in the chair. "Never again will I trust any man enough to sidetrack me from my goal. I don't care if it takes the next five years, the Emerald Light Cafe will open for business. I swear it."

After studying Doone for a moment, Marta placed her hands on the table. "My friend, life is like an herb which to rub between your fingers." She rolled her thumb and index finger. "You must take a chance to experience its, how do you say, piquancy. You pray it is pleasant, that it fills your nostrils with something less than a sting. It might make your eyes water, but it might make you smile. Laugh. Maybe cry. But pinch it you must, or what do you have but a life with no flavor."

Doone sniffed and rubbed the crumpled tissue against her nose. "What is that? One of Joseph's old Hungarian proverbs or something?"

"No. I make it myself for you because you are a cook? You do understand?"

Doone felt the beginnings of an almost painful smile. The past week spent in bed had brought her no wisdom such as this. Only a headache. She had loved and lost, and in the end, she had learned, too.

The experience with Hunter Mackenzie had reached into her soul as deeply as any roots she'd hope to sink. If the kind of feelings she'd had for him never happened again, and, of course, they never would, at least she'd had them once in her life. She pushed out of the heavy, hand-carved armchair and went to her friend. "Yes, I do understand." Hugging the older woman, she whispered, "Thank you."

Doone felt Marta's cool hand patting her on the wrist. "Marta? Do you miss Joseph still?"

Marta nodded slowly. "He is dead seven years, but our love is still in my heart. Real love remains there forever." She reached for the coffee pot. "Now, what about your other job? How did this happen?"

Doone slid back onto the chair. "When I got there, the entire staff along with the manager came over to tell me how sorry they were to hear about the death of my aunt. Talk about humiliation. At that exact moment, Cam Ludlow walks in. Can you believe I'm telling you this?"

Bewildered still, Marta shrugged. "But why would you lie to me? Of course, I believe. But you never told me your aunt died."

"Because I didn't have an aunt. Mr. Shackley made that up when he called to tell them I wouldn't be into work last week. Anyway, Cam reminded me, in front of Firebirds' staff and manager, that I didn't have an aunt, that I *never* had an aunt and how, in the name of heaven, did I think I was capable of opening my own restaurant when I was under such a delusion. Cam suggested, that because of my 'bizarre behavior of late,' I should make an appointment with a psychiatrist. People were backed up waiting for tables by then and my manager was demanding to know what restaurant Cam was referring to. I told Cam what he could do with his idea. That's when I got fired.''

The older woman didn't try to stifle her laughter. "What about your old job with the advertising agency. Will they take you back?''

"If I move to Chicago. But I'm not leaving Seattle, I'm not running away. This is where I've chosen to live and work. Besides, I've already contacted a real estate firm in Boston to see about selling my property. They sounded very hopeful that it will sell soon.'' She stopped to blow her nose. "I think with the money from Shackley and some little job I can make it through until my Boston property sells. But, about the rent for this month.''

"Do not worry about the rent. Teach a few extra classes for me, that is all I ask. Now, go upstairs and get some sleep. Tomorrow you can worry about getting some job to keep you going along.'' Marta shrugged and shook her head. "I know you, and you will not let those turtles get you down.''

"Turkeys, Marta,'' Doone corrected.

Doone gave her friend an extra hug before she went upstairs to her own apartment. Slipping under her apricot comforter and burrowing into her feather pillow was her only thought, before she unlocked the door and pushed it open. Her heart skipped a beat when she saw the blinking red light on her answering machine. Without switching on the lamp, she reached across the desk and pressed the rewind button. It could be a message from . . . anyone. Hunter Mackenzie, for instance. As the tape was rewinding, she screwed up her face and rolled her eyes toward the ceiling. When would that reflexive sort of reasoning cease, she wondered testily? After all, it was probably only Cam Ludlow apologizing. Or Firebirds deciding they had to have her back. The machine clicked to a stop and Doone depressed the playback button.

"It's Helmsley Real Estate, Miss Daniels. Thursday, three thirty P.M., and we've just placed a sold sign on your property."

As the rest of the detailed message played back, Doone sank against the door frame and whispered a prayer of thanks. She closed her eyes, reflecting on the strange and swift turn of events. What would this moment have been like if Cam Ludlow had put the property up for sale when she'd asked. Most certainly, the property would have sold sooner and she would never have met Mackenzie. No. No more thoughts of him tonight. Tonight she'd been given back her future. She clicked off the machine and switched on the light. And he was in her thoughts again.

Mackenzie had never been here and yet, somehow, because of him this place was emptier. And somehow, so was the triumph she felt about the sale of the Boston property. With a long, drawn-out sigh, she rested a shoulder against the door, and began a slow perusal of her living room. She'd never thought of this place as a real home. Even the oil paintings done by her mother, and the oak bookcase her father had made, now piled high with cookbooks, hadn't quite achieved that feeling. Then there was that dismal attempt two months ago at creating those braided silk pillows on the sofa next to . . . Harry Shackley?!

"Congratulations on your sale," said Harry Shackley, tossing aside the Longacres racing form he'd been reading.

"How did you get in here?" she managed, once she'd caught her breath. The unmitigated gall to break into her apartment and then silently watch her until she discovered him. Slicing her hand through the air, she silenced him before he could reply. "Never mind, just get out. And forget you heard anything about the sale of my property. You're not getting one penny of that bounty back."

"What?" Then as if something funny had struck him, he laughed and patted the cushion next to him. "Come on, Doone, have a seat. Let's have a talk for old time's sake. What do you say?"

"Are you out of your mind?" She snorted indelicately as she slammed the door and reached toward the phone, fully intending to call the police. "For old time's sake I ought to—"

"Sit down," finished Shackley, a little less jovial now. "This is about Mac."

She turned toward the sofa, her heart hammering at his tone. "What are you talking about?" she asked anxiously. Then the image of Mackenzie in danger, bleeding, dying flashed through her mind. "Has anything happened?"

Shackley pulled a cigar from the inside pocket of his jacket. Then, in as delicate a gesture as she'd ever seen him make, he bit off the end, picked the brown fleck from his tongue, and replaced it with his cigar.

Doone hurried toward him. The man was incorrigible! Leaning across the coffee table, she jerked the cigar from his mouth. "Tell me, for God's sake!"

Shackley nodded, a thoroughly satisfied look now in his eyes. "You're still in love with him, aren't you?"

She threw the cigar to the coffee table and shoved a hand through her hair. "Will you just tell me what's happened?"

Shackley locked gazes with her for another nerve-racking moment. Just when she thought she would scream, he dipped his chin and spoke. "He's alive."

Sinking into the empty chair opposite him, she let out a sigh of relief. She was hot and cold and shaking all at the same time. He was alive. Thank God. And, yes, she still loved him.

Doone wearily rubbed her forehead. "Thank you."

She slowly began uncovering her eyes as the next thought occurred to her. Shackley wasn't the type of person who would deliver bulletins to Mackenzie's ex-lovers without a good reason. A mixture of fright and suspicion began vying for control as she sat upright in the chair. "Why did you come here?"

"I said he's alive, but I didn't say he was going to stay that way. His life is in danger, Doone. That's why I'm here. The drug dealer he's to meet with has found out he's a government agent. Mac's got to be warned."

"Then why are you here? Why aren't you over there warning him?" she demanded.

"I've made too many trips into Portugal in the last

year. I can't take the chance that my own cover isn't already blown.'' He leaned to retrieve the cigar.

''Well, then someone from the embassy ought to warn him. That's the way these spy things are done, right?''

''Wrong. That's even worse than my attempting it. Headquarters found a leak in our Lisbon embassy office which wipes the staff and their contacts right off the board.'' Shackley glanced at his watch and straightened his tie. ''Look, I'll be straight with you. I need a fresh face in there for a few weeks, someone pretty. Someone Luis would have no knowledge of— I need you to do this. And we don't have much time.''

To do what? Rush into a situation she'd only read about in spy thrillers or seen in James Bond movies? Of course, James Bond girls were, like Christina, glamorous. Not to mention schooled in the martial arts. She blinked and shook her head, not quite believing that for a moment she was actually considering . . . My god, this was no romp through Jamaica. If what Shackley was telling her were true, this was Mackenzie's life. That Mackenzie didn't love her, was insignificant. She loved him and she wanted him to live. ''You *are* out of your mind. I don't know the first thing about this kind of job. Get someone from your Washington office. Someone with enough training to handle this properly.''

''There's no handling needed, Doone. Just tell Mac his cover's been blown and then do exactly what he tells you.'' Harry glanced at his watch.

There had to be more he wasn't telling her. He was a little too glib tonight, even for Harry Shackley.

She noticed beads of perspiration slipping down from his sideburns. "What's really going on? Won't they trust you with another Christina? Is that why you're here recruiting a dewy-eyed civilian?" She watched the cigar between his teeth freeze motionless.

Shackley tugged the cigar from his mouth, his jowls shaking with anger. "I had you pegged higher than just another jealous honey. Look, doesn't it matter that Mac's about to have his insides decorating the walls of a Portuguese grotto?"

Doone bolted from the chair, inflamed that he would accuse her of such a tactless act of jealousy and frightened beyond words that Mackenzie just might be on the brink of disaster. She began pacing the floor; Shackley was beginning to get to her. And it scared the hell out of her.

"How do I know you're telling me the truth?"

"You don't. That's why you're going to go."

"But why me? After I did everything I could to sabotage your efforts at getting him back into this business, you want my help? You want to take a chance with an untrained, unqualified person like me?"

"Wrong again. You came damn close to screwing me up when I was trying to get him to come back. Why? Because you turned out to have the best qualification of all. You're highly motivated, Doone."

She looked at him with disgust. "What are you talking about? Money?"

"Money's usually a good motivation. But you have a stronger one. Like I said, you still love him," he explained quietly.

"So did Christina," she shot back.

Doone waited for another snappy retort, but Shackley said nothing. She sat on the arm of her chair with her back to him. Was she motivated? Definitely. Capable? Maybe. But only maybe. Gullible? She balled her hands into fists and wrapped her arms around her waist. Mackenzie had certainly proven she was when he finally let her in on the fact that she didn't measure up to the memories of his dead lover.

"I said you loved him, Doone, not that you were obsessed with him. That was Christina's fatal flaw. You see, she—"

Doone felt an instant prickling at the base of her spine. How in God's name could he concoct stories on the spot about a dead woman? What a sick and twisted man he was. "Get out of here, Harry," she said, as she stood and moved toward the door. "You just lost. I may still have feelings for him, but I'm not stupid. Or gullible. If you'd lie about Christina, you'd lie about anything." She opened the door.

"Hold on."

"Whatever you're going to say, forget it. I don't know why you came here, and I don't want to know. I can't separate your fact from fiction, I never could." She watched as he stood up from the sofa and withdrew an envelope from his jacket. "I don't want your money or maps or whatever that is. Just leave."

"I didn't want to have to use this, but I see I'll have to."

He held out the envelope, but before Doone could look away she noticed the ragged opening along its top. Whatever the envelope contained, someone had opened it, probably Shackley.

"It's to you, from Mac," he began, stepping around the coffee table and coming toward the door. "He gave it to me before he left. You weren't suppose to get it unless he, uh, didn't make it back."

Mackenzie had written her a letter. *That kind of letter*. "Bastard," she whispered defeatedly to Harry as she took the envelope from him. She went into her bedroom, closed the door and stared down at the envelope through tear glistened eyes. EYES ONLY was stamped in magenta ink above and below her handwritten name. Her heart felt as if it were swelling in her throat as she slid the letter out and unfolded it.

"My Darling,

"Hopefully, you will never have to read this, but if you do, let me start by telling you how much I love you and how very sorry I am that I had to hurt you with that lie. No, Christina was never better than you—in any way. I told you that to make absolutely certain you wouldn't follow me. Believe me, darling. Close your eyes and remember us together, then ask yourself if what we shared wasn't love . . ."

She closed her eyes and did just that. Every sweetness, every passion-filled moment, every loving, laughing hour shared with him spilled through her mind.

He did love her. She should have known that he

was lying, even if she had no knowledge of why he would. Why had she so readily accepted his answer, then? She squeezed her eyes even tighter. Stupid! It was the old insecurity that had provided the impetus to ask him, "Was I as good as Christina?" It was the old fear that had hungrily accepted the answer, "No, you weren't."

After that moment, she opened her eyes and read on:

"I wasn't asleep last night when you were telling me you loved me. And knowing this, I was afraid you would have followed me to Portugal. Was I wrong to have figured it this way? I don't know, maybe I never will. The thing I do know is that I love you and I couldn't take the chance with the danger so great right now. I couldn't stand it if something happened to you. I'm so sorry I had to do it the way I did. I'll take that hurt in your eyes into hell with me.

"There is more I could try to explain to make you understand, but if you are reading this, then I am gone and the rest won't matter. Just remember, you were the best thing that ever happened to me.

HM"

She read it again, drinking in every precious word. He loved her and had never stopped loving her. She read it a third time. A sense of inevitability shot through her body like an exploding bullet. Mackenzie knew her so well. She *was* going to join him in

Portugal. He might die if she didn't go. And whatever else he had to explain, she would find out later.

She pulled open the drawer to her nightstand, reached into the back for the Space Needle earring and dropped it onto her lap. She removed the tiny gold studs and slipped the french hooked souvenir through her right earlobe. Kneeling on the floor, she reached under the bed for her suitcase. The Space Needle dangled against her neck, sharpening her awareness of Mackenzie's absence, and somehow, the danger he was in.

Shackley rapped on the door, then opened it. "Are you going?"

She slammed the suitcase onto her bed and then got to her feet. "Try and stop me," she said, pulling open a bureau drawer, scooping out an armful of clothing, and tossing it into her suitcase.

TEN

Doone set down her suitcase in the bustling lobby of the casino hotel in Albufeira, Portugal. This was where Mackenzie had managed the casino, where he'd made contact over a year ago with Luis, where he must have spent time with Christina. She rubbed her hands across her face and sighed loudly. Those surreal sensations usually accompanying jet lag were already beginning, but that was the least of her concerns. Harry Shackley had said that tonight was to be Mackenzie's first contact with Luis in a year. It was already late afternoon; she had to find Mackenzie fast. If only she hadn't missed the earlier connecting flight from Lisbon! She dragged her suitcase around a group of chattering tourists and over to the reception desk.

Harry had also said the first hurdle would be contacting Mackenzie inside the hotel. Mackenzie would have requested privacy and since most would remember him as their former casino manager, the staff would certainly oblige him. Her heart was rattling against her ribcage. If she couldn't warn Mackenzie in time, if she were already too late . . . Glancing at her watch through gritty eyelids and quickly calculating the time change, she winced. Drastic situations called for dramatic measures. Shoving her fingers through her hair, she hesitated a second, then proceeded to unbutton the top three buttons of her jump suit. *Only for you, Mackenzie.* Moistening her lips, she leaned an elbow on the counter and prayed for a randy desk clerk.

"Excuse me?"

The desk clerk looked up from his paper work and smiled appreciatively at what he saw. "How may I be of service to you?"

Gazing directly into the young man's eyes, she returned his smile with an easy one of her own. "I'm looking for a Mr. Mackenzie. What is his room number, please?" She gave a toss of her head allowing the tumble of curls to scatter indiscriminately around her shoulders and across her cleavage.

The clerk shuffled his papers, pursed his lips, and fought hard to stare over her head. "Mackenzie? Mackenzie? I'm afraid I don't—"

Doone reached to cover one of his hands with hers. Her gaze swept to the people climbing the staircase to the second floor casino and her voice was a breathy whisper as she hurriedly spoke. "Please! You know how he appreciates discretion."

The clerk's eyes widened for an instant, then his gaze wandered over her face and down to the swell of her breasts. "Ah. You say he is expecting you?"

"Yes, he is. Didn't he leave word about me? Miss Daniels?" Before he could reply, she shrugged.

"Well, my feelings aren't too hurt." She rolled her eyes toward the ceiling chandeliers. "You know how busy Mac is."

Patting the buttons of his jacket, he leaned across the counter. "Oh, all the time. In fact, he's been in and out all day. He went out again a short while ago."

Doone felt a stinging sensation through the center of her heart. Out? Had she missed him? Had he already left for the meeting with Luis? She twisted around, searching the lobby, hoping for a miracle. Hoping he would suddenly appear through the thickening knots of people. She couldn't have come all this way only to lose him now.

"Please. Do not worry. Mac will be back within the hour."

She whirled around, her hand flattened against her exposed cleavage. "Are you sure?"

"Absolutely."

"Thank God. I mean, this way I can surprise him." With a joy she couldn't have contained if she'd wanted to, she laughed out loud and squeezed the young man's hand. "Help me surprise him," she whispered.

Maybe this James Bond stuff wasn't so difficult, she decided, dropping her suitcase inside Mackenzie's sparsely but elegantly appointed suite five minutes later. Filmy, floor-length draperies covered two walls' worth of sliding glass doors, doing little to disguise the seductive glimmer of the Atlantic Ocean beyond. She hurried out onto the balcony and leaned against the rail. From this vantage point, she could see the parking lot, the front entry garden, and a myriad of narrow streets winding throughout the town. She'd be able to see him the moment he neared the building. She clicked her nails against the decorative tiles adorning the surface below the railing.

Waiting! How she hated waiting.

Slipping the french hook Space Needle earring from her ear she rolled it between her fingers. It was going to bring them luck, she told herself reaching up to rub a tickle on her neck. She jumped back, swatting wildly. *God! Was it some hideous bug? A gun!*

A hand closed over her mouth and she was dragged backwards before she could get out a scream. The crude laughter from three strangers around her sent an icy shockwave through her. She'd never been so terrified.

One man held her arms behind her back while a second, raising a gun, stepped forward and dragged the barrel underneath her jaw. Ending the slow traverse with a slight jam against her earlobe, he spoke in a frighteningly friendly manner. "So, you are Mac's new whore."

If this were only a simple robbery . . . but she knew better. The one holding her tightened his grip causing her to drop the earring and wince with fresh pain. "Who are you? What do you . . . want?" she asked. *Mackenzie, where are you?*

"I ask the questions." He ran his fingertips over her cleavage, then casually put his hand in his pocket. She hadn't thought to button the jumpsuit and it was impossible to do so now with both her arms held tightly to her side.

"Did Mac send you down from Lisbon? And where is Mac?"

"I'm just a . . . friend . . . from Seattle," she explained. Mackenzie's too late friend, she thought dejectedly. She had failed. There was no way to warn him now.

She watched as the third man emptied her purse, picked up her passport, and gave it to the man with a gun. He flipped through it quickly, then looked her over with a sly smile.

"No. I am his friend. Luis. And you, Miss Doone Daniels, are his whore." Luis tossed the passport back to the third man and placed the gun to the side of her head once more. "Where is he?"

She made an attempt to shake her head, but the gun slipped under her eye. "I don't know, I swear, I don't know. He doesn't even know I'm h-here. Yet." She closed her eyes and felt sick to her stomach. God, what was she doing? Leading Mackenzie right into a trap! "Actually, he's gone. He flew up to Lisbon and I don't know when he'll be back."

A short conversation ensued between the three men. The third man shoved everything back into her purse and put it and her suitcase under the bed. They were removing any trace of her ever having been there and she shivered at the possible implications of that.

Nudging her chin upwards with the gun barrel, Luis spoke softly. "You are lying. He doesn't know you have come, does he? Stupid woman. You are as stupid as his dead whore, following him around like this. Come, you are going with us."

The man holding her, gave her a shove towards the door and pulled out a gun. She stumbled slightly.

"Wait. Where are you taking me?"

Luis gestured toward the balcony. "There is a full moon tonight. I insist you take a boat ride along the Algarve's coastline and visit one of its grottos. People come from all over the world to gaze at the sand colored cliffs that glow in the moonlight. Then they beg the fishermen to take them through one of the tunnels into the grottos. Very dramatic, very romantic. But you won't have to beg." He smiled at his associates and made an obscene gesture Doone understood immediately. The two men laughed. "Isn't that what you want? A romantic, dramatic reunion with Mac?"

She had to stall them. Once she'd left the hotel, once they got her out on the ocean anything could happen. And none of it good.

"W-why can't we wait here for Mac?"

Luis smiled thoughtfully and she took a shaky little breath. He must be considering it. There, that wasn't so difficult. She buttoned her jumpsuit to the hollow of her throat. She'd get out of this alive yet, but only if she kept a cool head and thought logically. Ask logical questions. She wiped the perspiration from her upper lip. Maybe Mackenzie—

Luis closed the balcony doors and turned to face her. He sighed as if he were about to indulge a stubborn child.

"Wait here? And get blood on this beautiful carpet? You spoiled American women are a curious lot. Besides, the grotto holds so many wonderful memories."

*   *   *

Hunter Mackenzie entered the lobby and, as he had done on three other occasions that day, compared the time displayed on his digital watch to the time on the big brass wall clock. Two more hours until he'd be able to deal with Christina's murderer. This time he wanted no chance for slip-ups. He'd planned his moves with the complete cooperation of the Portuguese authorities. Time, logistics, manpower, all three insured the probability that Luis would be out of circulation and in custody well before midnight. And then it was home to Doone for a second chance.

Lone wolves ended up alone if they ended up alive. He allowed himself a hint of a smile. He intended to go on living and not alone, if Doone would listen and understand.

He approached the lobby's reception desk and asked for his messages. He was feeling lucky and even the unsuspecting clerk was winking conspiratorily as he handed Hunter an envelope.

"This was left here about half an hour ago, Mac."

Hunter opened the envelope, took out a slip of paper, and scanned it. It was a brief and final confirmation from Luis that they would meet as planned. Hunter began to walk away, but a nagging little voice inside made him hesitate. Nagging little voices, again. Intuition, prescience, and those damn little voices. He gave in to a good, heaving sigh. He always felt like a parapsychology experiment gone awry right before a meeting. But living life on the edge had taught him never to ignore the phenomena.

He turned back to the desk clerk. "Are you certain there are no other messages?"

The clerk hesitated. "Mac, you will take her fun away."

A cold, prickling sensation slid down his spine. "*Her* fun?"

"A very pretty lady who says she knows you well. Big blue eyes. And those sun dots on her nose. Freckles you call them, correct?"

Hunter never answered. With his heart somewhere in the vicinity of his stomach, he shoved Luis' note into his pocket and headed for his suite.

It couldn't have been Doone, he told himself. But even as he unlocked his door and flung it open he was calling her name. There was no answer and for a moment he slumped back against the door frame and lowered his head. It was then that he spotted Doone's earring, the earring he had given to her that afternoon at the Public Market in Seattle. He lifted it off the rug and stared at it. And those nagging little voices began to scream.

Luis had her.

It had been too early for moonlight an hour ago, when Luis motored her and his two men down the coast and into the grotto. Leaning back against the rough rock wall, Doone sat crosslegged in the damp sand waiting, and watching Luis and his men. They were playing a game of dice—for her. Each time one of the men cheered, her spirits sank a little lower. Like a wrapped prize, perched and waiting, she thought.

She looked beyond the men towards the deep green water filling most of the grotto, and then her gaze strayed to the opening in the craggy, cathedral-like ceiling above Luis and his men. Thin, orange light filtered down through the hole to barely illuminate the three men sitting around the overturned box. It would be dark soon, but she could still make out the three guns on top of the box. She strained to see the small open boat that had brought them. The boat was the only chance for escape. If there was some way she could . . . something moved. She squinted hard at the boat for one full minute, then quietly slouched back against the wall. The extra movement must have been the altered wave action from the incoming tide.

Her wrists were aching from the cord tied snuggly around them and the corners of her mouth were burning from the tight gag. All the same, when Luis and his men weren't looking her way, she struggled to free her hands. But she wasn't going anywhere and she knew it.

Luis looked at her, caught her eye, and took up one of the guns from the top of the box. He raised it at Doone, then pointed it above his own head. "His whore, Christina, was very stupid. She came in through there and was climbing down the rock when I shot her. She fell all the way to the sand. Boom."

The men's laughter made the skin on her spine crawl. Biting down on the gag, Doone inhaled the cool, damp air as deeply as she could. Mackenzie would come. There *was* a safe way out, there had to be. One way or another she wasn't going to die here, and neither was Mackenzie. One more time, that's all she was asking. One more time to look into those nickel gray eyes and whisper how much she loved him and how sorry she was to make such a mess of his plans.

Luis and his men were laughing again, the frightening sound amplifying as it echoed off the walls of the cave. She avoided their stares and instead focused on the last of the daylight glimmering on the surface of the water passing through the tunnel from the ocean. Mackenzie wouldn't have a chance motoring through that tunnel. Luis and his men would have their guns trained to the spot at the first sound. And there was at least twenty five yards of open water between the tunnel and this beach. Blinking back the tears, she narrowed her eyes and felt her heart plummet to her stomach, then rebound into her chest. There was something there, something. . . . Two, now three heads were bobbing, barely visible in the disappearing light. Heads. And face masks. That wavy hair *had* to be Mackenzie's. *Go back. They have guns. They're waiting for you, darling. Please, please, go back!*

"Mac is late," Luis called to her across the twenty feet of sand separating them.

The growing hope that the men in the water would remain undetected froze dead in her chest. Luis must have seen them. She twisted toward Luis and his men as he was clicking on a flashlight, shining it directly into her eyes. He shifted the light, placing it in the sand with the beam spreading down the beach. "Listen for his motor. Keep watching for him," he taunted her.

Luis *hadn't* seen the three scuba divers before they disappeared below the surface again. Hope welled in her chest. A film of perspiration broke out on her forehead. Mackenzie was here and Luis didn't know it. But how long could that last?

That part was up to her.

Don't look at the water, she told herself. Look at Luis. Stand up slowly. Don't look at the water. Atavistic commands for survival seemed to shout from some deep area in her brain. She must get Luis's attention and hold it away from the water, away from Mackenzie. *And she mustn't look at the water.* She struggled to her feet.

Luis placed his gun on the box next to the other two. "Where do you think you're going? You can't escape." His strident laughter filled the cave.

Forcing a dazed look into her eyes, she stared at Luis. She took a step backwards and felt the sheer rock against her back. All three men were on their feet and coming towards her, laughing at her jerky movements. Inching sideways along the rocks, her carefully studied movements drew the laughing, gunless men closer to her and away from Mackenzie and the other scuba divers. Let Luis and his men think they had her insane with fear and grunting through the gag for mercy. A bolstering feeling of recaptured control surged through her as she picked out the growing silhouettes of three scuba divers quietly making their way to shore. She stumbled once, then regaining her balance stepped up on a lump of sandstone. Pressing back against the cave wall, she moaned dramatically, hoping the sound would muffle any noise Mackenzie and his men might make. It felt good to *do* something.

Luis reached her and tugged the gag from her

mouth. "Guess which has won you first?" he whispered, pawing the front of her blouse.

"Mackenzie will kill you for this."

Luis's laughter stopped abruptly as it began. "Mac won't live long enough. That bastard played me for a fool last year leaving me to think we lost our connection over a jealous and overly imaginative whore. I was very angry when I found out who Mac was, and what he really wanted. Nobody plays me for a fool and gets away with it."

Luis's henchmen closed in around her, and she knew one more deep flash of terror when she lost sight of the water from her peripheral vision. Then she remembered Mackenzie and realized these few agonizing seconds would give him and his men time to better position themselves. With her tied hands pressed to her chest, she met Luis's menacing look and returned it with as much defiance as she could muster. "Get your filthy pigs away from me," she shouted, right before kicking solidly into the closest henchman's groin, sending him sideways into the second man. The two men stumbled to the sand. Luis's hand contacted smartly with the side of Doone's face, sending a shower of red-hot stars in front of her eyes. He drew a knife from his belt, bringing the flat side of it against her throat.

Not in his wildest nightmares had Hunter ever imagined this scene, not Doone with Luis and his men. Not the hope of his future at the mercy of a murderer from his past. He couldn't lose her. He wouldn't.

Suddenly she did something and the two henchman crumpled to the sand. Hunter reached inside his wet suit and pulled out the gun. He tossed his face mask aside, planted his feet wide apart in the ankle-deep water and brought his other hand up to the gun. "Step away, Luis. Now!"

Luis suddenly jerked Doone down from the rock and whirled her around. Pressing her against him for a shield, he spoke. "I think not, Mac. Look, she is already bleeding. Drop your weapons."

She heard the guns hit the water. It was the tiniest of cuts producing only a mild sting near her collar bone. Probably accidental at this point, Doone realized, but the next time Luis would mean it. She cast a side glance towards Luis's men. Dazed with surprise, they awaited his instructions.

"Too bad, Mac." Luis continued dragging her with him toward the box with the three guns. "This whore is much more clever than your last one, but not clever enough. She will have to die, too."

Hunter's heart lodged in his throat, his hands hanging empty, useless at his sides. Not twice in a lifetime, he prayed. God, not her, not Doone. He stood rigid and waiting, watching Doone's terror-brightened eyes and mechanical movements. *Be brave, my darling.*

"I love you, Mackenzie," she said and the lump in Hunter's throat grew larger. Hunter didn't dare take his eyes from hers. She might move, might see his man on the other side of the boat, and might scream.

He forced the lump back down his throat before he spoke. "What do you want, Luis? Just let her go and you can have it all. Safe passage. The drugs, the money, anything. Just let her walk away." The

soft roar of the ocean outside the grotto swelled painfully in his ears.

Luis wrapped his other arm around Doone's waist
and pulled her closer. "How touching. Two lovers
about to die and only one with the sense not to pretend otherwise. Stay where you are, Mac, and tell
your men to do the same or I'll slice her now."

Luis leaned toward the box to retrieve his gun at
the exact moment a blinding deluge of light hit them
from above. As Luis jerked into a reflective crouch,
Doone punched upward and away, breaking free. Her
near perfect movement ended in a splashing sprawl
onto the shore. Instinct told her to keep rolling even
when she'd caught sight of Mackenzie's fourth man
appearing from the other side of the boat and firing
his gun at Luis. The third roll sent her into Mackenzie's shins and subsequently, the shelter of his arms
as he reached to drag her to her feet.

"Watch out for the knife!" she shouted to Mackenzie.

"He's down, Luis is down." He felt her sag in
his arms, released from Luis's terror at last.

She was vaguely aware of the scuba divers over-
powering Luis's henchmen, of Mackenzie's instructions in Portuguese to the man who'd shot Luis, and
of uniformed policemen descending rope ladders
from the hole above. But it was Mackenzie that held
her spellbound. Mackenzie, whole and here. With
her wrists still tied, she pressed the back of one hand
to his cheek and looked into his eyes. Their steely
brightness told her just how concerned he'd been.
"I'm all right now," she assured him.

"You're bleeding," he said, drawing back and gently examining the small cut near her collar bone.

"He just nicked me with the knife when he turned. Hold me, Mackenzie. Hold me close and don't let go."

With a rush of emotion that took her breath away, he pulled her back into his arms. "I love you," he whispered, his voice cracking. His mouth came down to claim hers in a mingling of sweet relief and fiery desperation. She basked in his husky admission and the heat of his mouth as it moved over hers. They were safe and together.

"Untie me, Mackenzie. If I can't hold you soon I'm going to scream."

He untied her wrists, then stripped himself of the scuba equipment and wet suit. Her arms went around him and she held him close, savoring his cool flesh and the strong, steady beat of his heart. "At first I prayed for you to come and get me, but at the last moment, I hoped you wouldn't. Mackenzie, if you'd come by boat I would have lost you." She felt his arms tighten around her as she buried her face against him.

After a long while he lifted her head. "Let's get out of here and let these men finish up."

He spoke in Portuguese to one of the men he'd entered the grotto with. For a moment Hunter stared silently at Luis's body and then looked at Doone.

"Mackenzie?"

Hunter stepped in front of the body, blocking her view then stared solemnly into her eyes. "What is it, darling?"

"Maybe it wasn't the smartest thing she ever did,

but I understand why Christina came here that night. I understand because I love you, too. When Shackley finally had me convinced that your life was in danger, there was nothing or no one that could have kept me away. You understand, don't you?"

Kissing the cord-reddened flesh of her wrists, he nodded. "Yes." He reached into the hidden pocket of his bathing suit and brought out an earring. "When I found this in my suite my heart nearly stopped." He gave her the earring and she slipped it back into her earlobe. "When I think what could have gone wrong tonight, and if this scuba plan hadn't been prepared days ago . . ." His eyes softened and he touched her near the nicked flesh. "I could have lost you, too," he whispered. For a long moment he stared at her, then he took a deep breath and his voice became less emotional. "I was so proud of the way you kept your head and distracted them like you did. Have you been practicing that move to use on Harry?" he asked, trying to lighten the mood.

"Harry gave me your letter. He used it to get me here to warn you that Luis had found out you were working under cover."

Hunter closed his eyes and slowly shook his head. "I found that out about six hours after I arrived," he explained quietly, before opening his eyes. He steered her around the body and helped her onto the first rung of the ladder.

"Mackenzie, what's going to happen to Harry?" she asked, curious still for details that would complete the explanation.

"At the very least, he won't be retiring with a

totally successful score card, I'll see to that. Involving you was unprofessional, dangerous, and just plain stupid. He'll be lucky if the comptroller doesn't dock his pension. Let's get out of here, I'm freezing.''

Once up out of the grotto they were met by a group of policemen. A number of official vehicles with their lights flashing surrounded the area. Hunter spoke briefly to one of the policemen, then turned back to Doone to explain what was happening.

''We were prepared for anything tonight as you can see by the support vehicles and the extra police. The captain is going to let us have one of the ambulances to get us back to the hotel.''

''Ambulance?''

Hunter was already leading her through a small grove of olive trees towards one. He opened the back doors, dismissed the medics inside, and helped Doone in.

''But we don't need an ambulance,'' she protested.

Smiling, he climbed in after her and shut the doors. He slid open the small window behind the driver's head, gave him instructions, then closed the window and pulled the small curtain across it. Finally he turned to Doone and whispered loudly, ''Of course we need an ambulance. We haven't played doctor in a long time.''

He insisted on cleaning and bandaging her wound, while apologizing profusely during the procedure for any discomfort he might be causing her. He insisted she look out the window while he worked. As the ambulance made its way along the winding road high above the ocean, she saw the edges of the escarpments coated in golden light, and that same light dribbling across the water below. She was at once reminded of Luis. Luis might have lived to be interrogated if she hadn't been there. She looked back at Mackenzie who was moving about the ambulance, unfolding blankets and rearranging pillows for her like a mother hen. Then again, it might have been Mackenzie lying dead on the beach below, or even her. Closing her eyes, she dismissed the last two thoughts as quickly as she could. "Shouldn't we be going to a police station to fill out forms or something?"

Wrapping a blanket around both of them he pulled her into his arms and kissed her softly. "Tomorrow will be soon enough for that. When I get you back to my suite, I'm putting you in a hot bath. Then I plan on putting you straight to bed."

"Plan," she murmured, not able to meet his eyes. "You had other plans, didn't you? Harry said you were back for good. That once you'd captured Luis and questioned him, you'd know who the head of his organization was. Maybe if I hadn't been here—"

Hunter pulled away. "Since when have you believed anything Harry Shackley says? Never mind that question. Just look at me."

Reluctantly she lifted her gaze to the warmest smile she'd ever seen and a tremendous weight began lifting from her heart. "You're coming home?"

He gave her a mind-boggling kiss. "Of course, I'm coming home."

"You're sure you won't miss all—"

"Doone," he cut in quickly, "I had no intention of going undercover for any longer than it took to get Luis. The only reason I agreed to come here was to avenge Christina's death. I owed her that much. She was a loyal friend, someone I had depended on for a long time."

Doone shifted partly away from Mackenzie. "A friend?"

For a moment his gaze broke from Doone's and he appeared lost in sad memories. "She seemed so level-headed and cautious, but that all changed when she fell in love with me. Or, rather, when I told her that I didn't love her back. After that, she fell apart—"

Doone stared at him, totally flabbergasted. If he hadn't loved her, what *had* kept him isolated this last year?

"What's wrong? Are you in pain? Is everyth—" Hunter began.

Doone grabbed for his shoulders. "You didn't love her? Mackenzie, what were you doing on Eagle's Island for the last year, if you didn't love Christina? If you weren't grieving for her, what were you doing?"

"It was guilt, not grief."

"Guilt? But you didn't kill her. Luis killed her."

"I was in charge of the operation, and, therefore, responsible for her life. I should have seen just how serious her obsession with me had become by then. With her jealousy she'd even conjured up imaginary lovers and secret trysts for me; she had lost all sense of reality. Her last words were, 'Why couldn't you have loved me?' That's when the guilt and the 'what ifs' began." He cupped his hands around Doone's face and smiled. "You once asked me if I'd ever been in love. For months after she died I had wondered if I could have made myself love her, but by then love had become a dirty word. Then you showed up and no matter how hard I tried, I couldn't make myself not love you. That's when I realized that no matter how hard I could have tried with Christina, I couldn't have loved her because I was never meant to love her. I was meant to love you. Love," he said, stopping to kiss her, "has its own perfect plan."

The ambulance turned into the back portico of the hotel and squealed to a stop. Life had never been more precious, or more promising. Capturing his hand, she planted a kiss in his palm. "Hunter, I don't think I could love you any more than I do this very moment."

The ambulance driver opened the back doors, instantly breaking the intimacy of the moment for both of them. Hunter winked, then gave her the most tantalizing smile she'd ever seen. "Oh, I wouldn't be so sure of that. Just wait until I get you upstairs."

Later in bed, Hunter gingerly touched the edge of the second bandage he'd had to apply to Doone's knife wound. Looking at her lying in his arms, he winced with imagined discomfort. "You're sure we didn't hurt it in the tub?" he murmured, placing tiny kisses around the bandage.

"Very sure." The bath had been wonderful, especially since she'd shared the last half of it with him. She smiled wickedly, remembering how easy it had been to pull him into the bath water fully clothed.

And how much fun they'd had removing them. "Everything feels better since that bath. We work well in tight spaces, don't we?"

Lifting his mouth from the top of her breast, he raised his eyebrows in a comical leer. "Hmmm, you'd better change the subject, pretty lady, or before you know it we'll be rebandaging your wound again."

She pushed up on one elbow, shoved a lock of hair behind her shoulder and squeezed his arm. "Work! That reminds me. I finally have the money for the Emerald Light Cafe." She gave him a wry little smile. "Now all I have to do is find a location. As you can imagine, I was too late for—-"

"Oops, before I forget," he interrupted. "I have a message for you."

Doone sat up with a start. "Me? But who knows I'm here in Portugal?"

Hunter touched the tip of the Space Needle earring dangling wildly from her sudden movement and nodded. "An ex-hermit. He says he knows the perfect site for your restaurant. It's right in his inn overlooking Puget Sound. And he says you're perfect for the job."

"He does?" It was more of a statement than a question as she fought back a bubble of laughter. "Why is that?"

Hunter touched the earring. "He loves . . . your taste in cheap jewelry."

She reached up to close her fingers around his. "Any other reason?"

"He loves . . . your cooking? Says he'll only take

you on if you're willing to make it a family restaurant, though.''

"Family restaurant? Well, he'd better be willing to make it legal. Is twenty-six too old to be adopted?''

"Adoption?'' He broke into laughter as he pulled her back into his arms. "That's not part of his plan, lady.'' Suddenly his playfulness disappeared and a soft and serious look came into his eyes.

Doone looked him over quietly. The moonlight was spilling across his hair and bathing his face and shoulders in purest platinum. The perfection of the moment swelled in her heart. "And just what is his plan?'' she whispered.

Sliding her down on the bed, he trailed a ribbon of kisses over her shoulder and into the hollow of her throat. "To marry you, because he loves you very much.''

She smiled up adoringly. "But I can't marry him, because I'm planning to marry you.''

He pulled back the thin sheet separating them, covered her body with his, and whispered against her mouth, "What a perfect plan.''

SHARE THE FUN . . .
SHARE YOUR NEW-FOUND TREASURE!!

You don't want to let your new books out of your sight? That's okay. Your friends can get their own. Order below.

No. 7 SILENT ENCHANTMENT by Lacey Dancer
She was elusive and beautiful. She was Alex's true-to-life princess.

No. 29 FOSTER LOVE by Janis Reams Hudson
Morgan comes home to claim his children and finds Sarah who claims his heart.

No. 30 REMEMBER THE NIGHT by Sally Falcon
Levelheaded Joanna throws caution to the wind and finds Nathan just isn't her fantasy but her reality as well.

No. 32 SWEET LAND OF LIBERTY by Ellen Kelly
Brock has a secret and Liberty's freedom could be in serious jeopardy!

No. 33 A TOUCH OF LOVE by Patricia Hagan
Kelly seeks peace and quiet and finds paradise in Mike's arms.

No. 34 NO EASY TASK by Chloe Summers
Hunter is wary when Doone delivers a package that will change his life.

No. 35 DIAMOND ON ICE by Lacey Dancer
Diana could melt even the coldest of hearts. Jason hasn't a chance.

No. 36 DADDY'S GIRL by Janice Kaiser
Slade wants more than Andrea is willing to give. Who wins?
